HEART OF ICE

(HEARTS ON FIRE, BOOK 1)

ROBIN BRANDE

RYER PUBLISHING

HEART OF ICE
(Hearts on Fire, Book 1)
By Robin Brande

Published by Ryer Publishing
www.ryerpublishing.com
Original Copyright 2012 by Elizabeth Ruston/Robin Brande
Revised Edition Copyright 2014 by Robin Brande
www.robinbrande.com
All rights reserved.
Cover photo Dreamstime.com
Cover design by Robin Ludwig Design, Inc.
www.gobookcoverdesign.com

❋ Created with Vellum

BOOKS BY ROBIN BRANDE

<u>Romance</u>

Love Proof

Right On Time

Freefall

Heart of Ice

Fire and Ice

<u>Fantasy</u>

The Bradamante Saga

<u>Young Adult</u>

Evolution, Me & Other Freaks of Nature

Fat Cat

Doggirl

The Parallelogram Series

Replay

The Good Lie

<u>Nonfiction</u>

What If You're Doing It Right?

What If You're Doing It Right? For Teens

"It's not too late."

Annie smiled. "I'm going."

Her cousin Shannon took another bite of airport hamburger and shook her head. "I can't believe it. The first impulsive thing you do *in your life*, and you don't even invite me along."

Annie stole a cluster of fries. "Well? Want to come?"

"To the North Pole? No, thank you."

"It's not the North Pole. It's Iceland."

"Yeah, listen: *Ice*-land."

"It's a trick," Annie explained. "Greenland is ice, Iceland is green."

"I don't care. You'll freeze."

"The lowest it will be is forty degrees. I've got clothes for that."

"And not much else if that's all you're taking," Shannon said, pointing to Annie's single carry-on bag.

"I don't need much. I don't plan on going anywhere."

"Forty degrees? That's freezing for you. You hate the cold."

Annie shrugged.

"What," her cousin asked, "has gotten into you?"

"I'm just going," Annie answered. "I'm not going to worry about it."

Shannon shook her head. "I leave you alone for a week—"

"See? That's what happens when you go on vacation and don't write."

"They don't have e-mail in the woods."

"Your loss. I would have told you about it much sooner—yesterday, at least."

"Did you really just decide?" Shannon asked. "Just like that?"

"Yep. I know—it's not like me. Strange, huh?"

Shannon eyed her cousin skeptically. "Is there more to this than I know?"

"Like what?"

"It's the Mark thing, isn't it?"

"No, it's not."

Shannon raised one eyebrow. "Oh, that's right—I don't know you."

Annie couldn't help chuckling. Although she didn't see her cousin often enough anymore, Shannon was still like a sister to her. They had both grown up as the only girls in households full of boys. From the time they were infants until they graduated from high school they spent part of every summer together, a united front against their brothers, an exclusive two-girl club for sharing secrets and sympathy.

When Annie's mother died a few years ago, Shannon had taken the red-eye from Minneapolis to Phoenix, then rented a car and driven to Tucson, just to sit quietly by Annie's side and listen to her cousin cry. When Shannon's marriage had fallen into ruin, Annie flew up to help Shannon move to an apartment and rearrange the pieces of her life.

They were both 31 now, both single again. They shared their mothers' good looks: ivory skin, gray-green eyes, dark brown hair that Shannon kept in short, soft curls and Annie wore in a sleek page-boy cropped at the neck.

"So," Annie said, seizing control of the conversation, "did you have fun with...what's his name?"

"David. Fun, but not so fun."

"Not a camper, huh?"

"Not in the least."

"But I'm sure he has other fine qualities."

Shannon chewed thoughtfully. "Some."

"Shan, do you really think taking a guy backpacking for a week is a fair test of his qualities as a boyfriend?"

"Yes. How am I going to know if a man measures up unless I can see him make a campfire?"

"That's your brothers talking."

"But they have a point."

"So he failed the test, huh?" Annie asked.

Shannon jutted out her thumb and flipped it over. "Cute, but inept."

"Out he goes?"

"Out he goes." Shannon sat back and surveyed the gathering crowd of passengers. "Look at all these people," she whispered. "Iceland must be the land of the blonds. People are going to stare at you everywhere you go."

Annie scanned the ticketing area. It was true: Most of the people were fair-skinned and blond. "Good. Finally I'll get to look exotic."

"What do they speak there?"

"English. And Icelandic. And I think maybe Danish."

"What do you even know about this place?"

Annie held up her guidebook. "Everything I need to know for now."

"And someone's going to meet you?"

"I take a bus from the airport, then someone from the horse farm will pick me up where it lets off."

Shannon shook her head. She took another bite of burger. "And this horse farm thing. What's it called?"

"Saga Farm."

"Saga Farm, right. So where'd that idea come from? I thought you were afraid of horses. Every time I've tried to teach you, you hated it."

"I'll be fine."

"Yeah, but what if—"

Annie squeezed her cousin's knee. "Stop it—I mean it. I'm going, so be happy for me."

"I am happy for you," Shannon said, beating Annie to the last of the fries. "Of course I am. And I'm really proud of you. I know this isn't your kind of thing—a long plane ride—over an ocean, for heaven's sake—going to a foreign country—I mean, where have you ever been before?"

"Nowhere. That's the point."

"And going by yourself," Shannon continued. "I don't get that. Where'd all this come from?"

Annie shrugged. "I just decided I've been too afraid of things. I've been letting my life slip by."

"It's because of Mark. Admit it."

Annie sighed. "I don't know, maybe. I guess that was just the last thing that helped me decide I needed this. So that's good, right?"

"Yeah," said Shannon, "it's good you caught him groping Miss Biology in the teachers' lounge. It's good he's been cheating on you for who knows how long. It's good he's a—"

Annie held up her hand. "It doesn't matter," she said, hoping to convince herself. "It's over. I've moved on."

Shannon bit the inside of her cheek. "Can I just say I hope they'll be very miserable together?"

"I'm sure they will be."

"Listen, I know you don't want to hear this—"

"Then don't say it."

Shannon was never one to be put off. "I'm not excusing him—he's a complete bastard—but you should know that not every guy is willing to date someone for four months without some action."

"There was action."

"Not of that particular kind. Come on, Annie. Don't you think maybe there's such a thing as going too slow?"

"No."

"Hmm." She pretended to take great interest in the rest of her burger. "So what are you going to do about next year? Keep teaching there?"

"I don't know. I already told the principal I'll be renewing my contract."

"But school's not for a month and a half," Shannon said, "right? You can change your mind."

"And do what?" Annie asked. "I've been there longer than Mark has. I'm not leaving just because of him."

"But I thought you weren't happy there this year anyway."

Annie shrugged in resignation. "I don't know, Shan. I don't want to think about any of that right now. I want to go to Iceland. I want to be someplace where I have to wear a coat in the summer. I want to see where the Vikings lived and walk where they walked and learn to ride a horse and..." She leaned forward and whispered conspiratorially, "I just want to live a bigger life for once—you, of all people, can understand that, right?"

Shannon touched her forehead to her cousin's and whispered, "You bet."

WHAT AM I DOING? Annie wondered. She was three hours into the six-hour flight, her legs cramping, her mind spinning. *No going back. Just do this.*

No wonder Shannon thought she was crazy. Annie had called her just two days before and announced her plans. She would fly to Minneapolis, meet Shannon in the airport for a few hours, then keep going to Reykjavik, the capital of Iceland.

All because of a story. Annie had left out that part when explaining to Shannon her reasons for going. But the truth was, if not for coming across that story, Annie would still be home sweating through another Tucson summer and fuming over her ex-boyfriend's infidelity.

Someone had left the book out on the library table. She had never heard of the sagas of the Icelanders, but there they were, just a fraction of them collected in one thick volume. Annie had some vague impression of the Vikings and their exploits, but here were epic tales as absorbing as any of the Greek legends she had studied in college.

Hardy seamen and warriors and their even hardier wives. Women widowed and remarrying repeatedly as their men fell under sword or wave. Love affairs giving rise to blood feuds that spanned generations.

And there in the midst of the turmoil was the fearsome Freydis, illegitimate daughter to the Erik the Red, half-sister to the great explorer Leifur Erikson.

Pregnant, unarmed, the men in her party besieged by a band of warriors who had landed on their beach, Freydis erupted into action. She refused to give in to the inevitable slaughter. She charged down the beach toward the invaders, scooped up a sword from one of her fallen companions, and shouted with all the fury of a wild animal. She tore open her shirt and bared her swollen breasts. Now she had the warriors' attention. She beat the sword against her breast, screaming and cursing and threatening their very souls. The invaders fled to their boats and rowed away, Freydis's screams filling their ears.

Wow, Annie had thought. *Why can't I have that kind of fire?*

Sitting there in the library, the sagas open on her lap, she replayed the scene in the teachers' lounge.

I open the door. There's Mark, there's Sherry. His hand is hidden behind her. He looks up, sees me, pulls his hand away. They scoot away from each other and smile at me in that fake, guilty way.

I run to the coffee machine. Rip open my blouse. Pour scalding coffee on my breast...

Annie shuddered. *No, try again.*

I rip open my blouse. (Leave the lacy bra on—it's one of my favorites—no point in ruining it on his account.) Take the grammar book I'm holding and beat it against my breast while shouting—while shouting—

And there the fantasy ended. What could she have said? "I wasted four months on you! Die, fiend!" Words seemed inadequate. Maybe she'd done the only thing she could do under the circumstances: close the door and walk away.

He tried to lie, of course, but Annie knew. She realized she had known for weeks. She didn't love him, but hoped to if she gave it enough time.

Once again Annie wondered if it was really her fault, rather than any of the men she'd met. Yes, Mark was a bastard, just like Shannon said, but so what? What about any of the others she'd tried to talk herself into liking? Maybe there was something wrong with her. This kind of numbness inside her, this hollow in her chest that had only grown larger since her mother died.

Maybe that's why the Icelandic sagas had hit her so hard. Women like Freydis weren't numb. The women in those tales were passionate and angry and fierce. They loved so hard their men sometimes died from it. Nobody was living a half-life. Nobody was just watching their lives pass by, wondering if there was something missing that would help them feel more. Those people felt plenty, every second of the day.

So she'd done the unexpected. For once in her life been irrational. Gone home, done a bit of research, and booked her trip that very night. Then packed a single bag and left her home behind before she could think too hard about what she was doing.

She would play the part of heroine for once—bold, uncompromising, fearless. Maybe she would find a bit of Freydis's spirit somewhere in Iceland, and let the woman warrior fill the hollow in her heart.

The flight attendant moved through the cabin with a cart of duty-free items. Annie glanced at the jewelry on top. What she needed was a duty-free vacation—no obligations, no schedule, no one expecting anything from her. She closed her eyes and settled back into her seat for last three hours of her flight.

Kjartan Thorbjornson grunted his good mornings. Five riders stood waiting in the stable, their boots already muddy.

"You," Kjartan said, pointing to a gray-bearded German, "get a helmet." Kjartan surveyed the rest of the group. He could usually tell from the way they stood which ones were the novice riders. He picked out a British woman standing stiffly near the railing. He would assign her the slowest horse. The rest—he'd just have to see. He could switch around horses on the trail once he had a better sense of his customers' skill.

Kjartan's assistant Petra, a red-haired German woman in her late twenties who had been working for him on the farm for the past five summers, helped her countryman select a riding helmet. They muttered in low tones, deferring to Kjartan's preference for silence. When the man was properly capped, Kjartan said simply, "Good."

While Petra cinched the saddles and checked the bridles, Kjartan directed riders to their horses. "You, take that one. You, over here." The group was a mix of Germans and French and a Brit, with Kjartan the only Icelander. English was the group's common language. Although Kjartan, like all Icelanders, had learned English in elementary school, he still preferred using as few words of it as possible. Even when speaking Icelandic he was terse. No good had ever come from saying too much.

He was right about the British woman. She clutched her legs around the horse like she was straddling a high wall.

"Petra," he mumbled to his assistant, "that one's yours."

Petra nodded. She led her horse toward the woman's, then withdrew a tether from her coat pocket and clipped the two bridles together. "We'll go slow," Petra assured her. The woman nodded nervously.

Kjartan looked at his watch. He preferred to move through his day without ever looking at the time, but he didn't have that luxury today. He had three groups to guide before supper, and another one that night. In between he had supplies to pick up, a meeting with the vet who was coming out to check on one of the mares, and a new guest arriving at the bus stop.

In his e-mail confirming her registration, he'd promised someone would meet her with the van. Kjartan worked through the logistics as he turned his horse onto the trail. If he took this group across the short cut, he would just make the American's bus in time.

Americans. Why his ex-wife had been so fascinated with them, he still didn't understand.

In his eight years running a tourist horse farm, Kjartan had found Americans to be arrogant, self-involved, and condescending. More of them arrived every year as travel magazines touted the charm of Reykjavik and the country's exotic landscapes filled with volcanoes, glaciers, and towering waterfalls. One man—a tax attorney from Dallas—had actually told Kjartan he was disappointed the volcano looming over the farm hadn't erupted during his visit. Kjartan bit his tongue and nodded empathetically.

The ones who came to his farm had seen pictures of shaggy Icelandic horses and thought the "ponies" would be fun to ride. They had no appreciation for the horses' history as the original

Viking breed, kept pure for the last thousand years. He could count on one hand the Americans who knew anything about Iceland beyond the fact that the singer Björk was from there.

Because most Icelanders spoke English, the Americans made no effort to learn even the simplest Icelandic words. Those who had stayed at the farm expected world-class, 24-hour service, despite the fact that Kjartan did most of the work alone. Petra had worked for him over the past several summers—cooking, cleaning the cottages, helping him guide trips —but the bulk of the details still fell on Kjartan's shoulders.

Which was why he would have to find time to retrieve the American from the bus stop.

American or not, this one was traveling alone, and that posed its own burdens. Male or female, the solo traveler expected to be entertained, coddled. Kjartan had neither the time nor the patience.

He would make it Petra's job to keep this woman Annie out of his way.

2

Annie set her bag on the concrete outside the little grocery store where the bus had dropped her off. She checked her watch: 11:10 AM. The bus had left her there five minutes early. She sat on top of her carry-on bag, leaned against the wall, and closed her eyes. She was not going to sleep—this was just a long, slow blink. She would obey all the advice she read on the Internet and stay awake until her normal bedtime.

She awoke to a gentle nudge against her shoulder.

"Here for Saga Farm?" the man asked.

Annie nodded, disoriented. She pushed onto unsteady legs. "Sorry. What time is it?" She glanced at her watch.

Kjartan mumbled something. He reached for her bag and stowed it in the back of the van.

"I'm Annie. Are you Mr...." She waited, wanting him to pronounce it first. The name looked daunting in his e-mail— Thor-something—and she knew she would butcher it.

"Kjartan," he answered. "No 'Mr.'" He pronounced his first name in two syllables, K'YAR-tun.

Annie repeated it, trying to imitate the soft roll of the "r." "Would you say your last name for me?"

"Thor-B'YORN-son." Again, with the rolling "r's." It sounded lovely coming from someone who was a native speaker. Annie was sure her hard "r's" and flat American accent would not do it justice.

The idea of Icelandic surnames intrigued her. The guidebook explained that last names were based on a father's first name and the gender of his child. Women's names ended in "dottir," men's in "son." Instead of Linley, Annie's last name would be Alansdottir. Her brothers would be Alanssons. The guidebook pointed out the confusion Icelandic families generated when traveling abroad, since mother, father, and children all had different last names.

While she waited in the airport that morning for the bus to arrive, she had checked something else the guidebook mentioned. The phone book—a thin publication covering the entire population of the island—had listings by first name only. She scanned the pages: Gudrun Arnolfsdottir... Gudrun Magnus-dottir...Gudrun Sigurdardottir. Every now and then a clearly foreign name would pop out at her: James McKenzie (listed with the "J's"). Susan Jenkins, right after Solija Olvikdottir.

Kjartan reached for her bag. He scanned the area around her. "Is this the only one?"

"Yes. I thought—well, I assume it's not fancy at the farm. No formal dinners or anything," she added, smiling.

"*Nei*. No formal dinners."

Kjartan opened the sliding door and offered Annie a hand up. Uncomfortable with the gesture, she ignored his hand and climbed in. When he was seated behind the wheel she asked, "How far is it?"

"Thirty minutes."

"Thanks for picking me up."

Kjartan seemed too absorbed by the sheet of paper on the seat next to him to answer.

"What's the weather been like?" Annie tried.

He lifted his eyes to the rear view mirror. "Not so good today. It was better last week."

She nodded, noting the rough gray clouds outside the window. "Will it rain, do you think?"

"*Já*." The word had a strange, round sound to it, a cross between "Yow" and "Yo." It sounded closer to "no" than "yes."

"No?" Annie repeated.

"Yes," Kjartan enunciated, clearly annoyed.

Annie settled back onto the seat. Fine. She wasn't here to make friends with every Icelander. The guidebook was right again: The people here were much more reserved than Americans. The book suggested she could get Icelanders talking if she approached them gently, but otherwise, she shouldn't expect much open interaction.

Right now she was too tired to care. In fact, she was grateful for the quiet. She closed her eyes—just for a few minutes—while the van glided down the road.

She awoke even more disoriented than before. She sat up and looked outside the window of the van. It was parked in the driveway of a two-story house. Equipment in various states of disrepair rested against the wall. Next to the house was a smaller structure she took to be the stables, since a line of people exited, towing their horses by the reins.

Annie noticed her seatbelt—which she always wore—was unbuckled. Her bag was gone, too. On the seat beside her was a key marked "4."

Annie ran a hand over her hair and swiped her sleeve across her mouth. She must look a mess. Who cares—she didn't know anyone there, and wasn't that part of the point? She could be whomever she wanted for the next two and a half weeks.

Coffee. Her body screamed for it. Her head ached from sleep deprivation and caffeine withdrawal. The guidebook had promised Iceland was a land of coffee addicts. Annie was ready to join them. She had no illusions about finding a Starbucks anywhere near, but she had the feeling the native brew could be even better.

She slid open the door to the van and stepped onto the soft dirt. The ground was slightly spongy, as though it were never completely dry.

She clutched the key in her hand and looked around for the cottages she had seen on the farm's website. To her right and down a foot path she saw them: four white wooden buildings that looked like small German restaurants. They had that same scalloped detail, the same flowery border painted on the edge of the eaves, that she had come to associate with bratwurst and sauerkraut. Shannon loved to drag Annie to the German restaurants in Minneapolis, where the two of them loaded their plates and suffered later through days of raucous indigestion.

Cottage number 4 was nearest the house. Annie climbed the two wooden steps onto the porch. Her bag was outside the door. She stood under the protective eave and slipped the key into the lock, then wrestled with the door. No luck. She backed up and checked the number on the front wall again, willing to believe her addled brain had made a mistake. No, number 4. Plus, she reminded herself, her bag was here.

Once again she tried to coax the door open, first pulling it toward her, then easing it away, all the while babying the key in the lock.

She paused to rest. This staying awake was too much for her. She hadn't slept in—what, almost 24 hours? She didn't count the stray cat naps she'd been taking every time she sat down. Annie concentrated her energy for one last try.

And broke the key in the lock.

"Great."

She stumbled down the steps back onto the foot path. A young woman passed her and smiled. Annie's reflexes were so slow she was unable to smile back before the woman was several feet down the path. Annie turned, curious. The young woman disappeared into the flaps of a faded blue two-person tent staked to the grass behind the house.

Campers. She had noticed tents all along the bus route—lone structures out in the middle of fields, a few clustered together near waterfalls and streams, half a dozen scattered throughout a designated campground. It was odd to see one set up so close to someone's house, but what did Annie know about the customs there? Maybe everyone in these remote areas let people camp on their property.

She continued walking toward the stables. She could see a few people milling about. "Excuse me," she called out, "is Kjartan there?"

None of them answered. The woman turned and said something to her male companion, who nodded. Another man looked at Annie blandly, then bent down to continue scraping mud from the side of his boot.

"He's away," said a voice behind Annie. She turned to find the young woman again. "Can I help you?" She added in a whisper, "I don't think any of them speak English."

"I need help with my door," Annie told her. "I broke off the key."

The young woman smiled warmly. "Ah! That happened to me once. Come inside. Let me see if I can find someone."

Her accent was faintly French, although Annie couldn't be sure. "Do you work here?" Annie asked.

"No, I am staying in the tent there, but they won't mind if we go inside."

She opened the door to the house without knocking. "Petra?" the young woman called. Casually she kicked off her boots and headed down the hall.

Annie followed.

"Oh, you need to take off your boots first," the young woman said.

Annie remembered reading something about that in the guidebook. "Right, sorry."

The woman smiled. "No problem. Are you American?"

"Yes. And you? French?"

"Yes." She held out her hand. "My name is Sophie."

"Annie."

"Ah, you're the woman who's come alone."

"Yes," Annie answered, a little surprised.

"This was a good place to come. You'll like it here."

"At the farm, or in Iceland?"

"Both."

Divested of her boots, Annie padded down the hall after Sophie. They entered a small kitchen taken up almost entirely by a long narrow table.

"Petra?" Sophie stepped into the room beyond the kitchen. "She must be out riding. Let me see what I can find."

She led Annie into a small office just beyond the kitchen. A computer, printer, fax machine, and telephone crowded the worn pine desk. A shelf above the desk held dictionaries: English, German, French, Danish, Italian. Photographs—some color, some black and white—covered every inch of space along the walls.

Sophie ran her finger along a row of keys hanging from a peg board.

"You are number four?"

"Yes. But a key won't help. I broke it off inside the lock."

Sophie scowled. Her pleasant features showed none the worse for it. Annie admired the natural beauty of French women. In college she had made a pilgrimage once a week to the small, dirty theater near campus where all the foreign movies came. She had taken French for two years in high school, and continued through college. She enjoyed comparing the subtitles to what her ear could pick up and translate.

She loved the images of French life: the outright femininity of the women, the easy charm of the men, the flirting and maneuvering that inevitably led to bed. Annie spent her college years a virgin, and took vicarious pleasure in watching the freedom with which the characters entangled themselves with one another. One woman might sleep with three or four men in a good French romp. The films didn't shy away from any of the details. Annie learned more from them than she did from reading romance novels.

She liked the way French women made themselves up: mascara on the upper lashes only, bright red lipstick, a subtle swipe of blush. They sat in cafés smoking, drinking coffee from large bowls. Although she couldn't imagine smoking, Annie was happy to embrace the coffee habit. She gave away her mismatched mugs and started drinking from her soup bowls instead. She started treating herself to what she considered a classic French breakfast, dipping jam-slathered toast into bowls filled with half coffee, half milk.

Annie smiled at the memory now. Sophie was the first real French woman she had ever met. And it was clear the young woman's beauty didn't come from clever makeup techniques or tight, inviting clothes. Her skin was clean and pale, her eyes a wide, friendly blue, her full lips curved in a perpetual smile. Her long brown hair was matted—almost dreadlocked—and gathered in a careless ponytail. She looked at Annie with such open friendliness, Annie couldn't help but smile back.

She also couldn't help but make the association between Sophie and those imitation French breakfasts from college.

"I could really use some coffee," Annie said. "Do you know where I can get some?"

"Yes, yes," Sophie answered enthusiastically. "I'm sure you need some. Did you fly last night?"

"Last night, this morning—I'm not sure which." Annie looked at her wristwatch. "Two o'clock here is..." She tried to picture the hands on a clock, running them backward seven hours to Arizona time. Her mind was moving so slowly...

"In Iceland, forget about time," said Kjartan. He leaned into the office and pulled a stack of papers from his desk. Then he stood in the doorway, searching through the papers, not looking at either woman.

"She needs help with her door," Sophie said.

Kjartan looked up. "Why? What's wrong?"

"I'm sorry," Annie said, "but I sort of broke the key off."

She expected to hear the same irritation in his voice as before. Instead, he went back to shuffling through his papers. "I'll take care of it. Just a moment."

Satisfied, Sophie turned to the next issue. "Coffee. Come with me."

Annie sat at the table while Sophie coasted confidently around the kitchen. She opened drawers, cupboards, assembled the supplies. She measured grounds from a yellow metal canister on the counter.

"How long have you been here?" Annie asked, registering the young woman's familiarity with the place.

"A week."

"Only a week?"

"Yes." Sophie turned to her with a smile. "Why?"

"It's just that—you act like you've lived in this house for a while."

"It's very casual," Sophie explained. "You'll get used to it."

With the coffee brewing, Sophie sat across from Annie. She

propped her elbows on the table and rested her chin on her hands. "Tell me everything."

Annie laughed. "Everything. Okay, I came to learn to ride Icelandic horses."

"You'll love them. They're beautiful."

"Do you ride?"

"Yes. Every day since I'm here—sometimes twice a day."

"Did you know how to ride before you came?"

"Yes. I have a horse of my own."

"Oh." Annie's confidence lagged. She leaned forward so Kjartan wouldn't hear. He still stood in the doorway to his office, shuffling through papers, apparently ignoring them both. "I've only ridden once or twice. I don't really know how."

"That's all right," Sophie whispered back. "You can learn."

"The guidebook says Icelandic horses are easy to ride—that beginners can learn in a day. Do you think that's true?"

Sophie pursed her generous lips. "Yes, maybe—in a way. It can be easy. It depends on what you want."

"What do you mean?"

"If you want to ride on a trail, you can walk along—no problem. If you want to go faster—"

"Definitely not," Annie said. "Slow is good."

"Then yes, probably," Sophie said. "You shouldn't have a problem."

The drip coffeemaker spewed out one last plume of steam. Sophie bounded from her chair and filled two mugs. "Milk?"

"Yes, please." Annie tried not to feel disappointed about the mugs. She almost asked Sophie if she drank coffee from a bowl at home, but decided that was foolish. Movies weren't real life. The French probably had all sorts of strange impressions of Americans based on the movies they'd seen.

Annie took her first sip of Icelandic coffee. It tasted slightly burnt, definitely stronger than she was used to. Rather than ask Sophie for more milk, she stood and went to the refrigerator herself. She was just pouring some more into her mug when Kjartan joined them in the kitchen.

Annie snapped the refrigerator closed and sat back down. She felt caught, somehow, a stranger helping herself to her host's food without permission. Sophie didn't seem a bit embarrassed. "What time will we go tonight?" she asked.

"Seven o'clock," Kjartan answered.

Sophie turned to Annie. "Will you go?"

"Where?"

"On a ride."

"At seven o'clock tonight? That's so late."

Sophie laughed. "Don't worry—it won't get dark."

"Right," Annie said, a little embarrassed. "I know that." The truth was, she had a hard time absorbing the concept of endless daylight.

"You should come," Sophie coaxed. She reached across the table and clasped Annie's hand. Normally Annie would have shied away from a stranger's touch, but Sophie's gesture was easy, natural, friendly. Annie smiled. The young French woman was irresistibly amiable.

Annie looked to her host for any hint that he thought she should come along. His face told her nothing.

"No," she told Sophie, "I think I'll be dead asleep by then. I'm going to try to stay awake as long as I can, but I'm really looking forward to going to bed tonight." She glanced again at Kjartan. "Thanks for not waking me in the van. I guess I needed that nap."

"*Já*. Okay." He jerked his chin toward Sophie. "See you tonight."

"See you," Sophie answered. She turned to Annie. "You'll go tomorrow. I'll show you what to do, okay?"

"Okay. Thanks."

Annie heard Kjartan greet someone before shutting the door behind him. Soon a young man wandered shoeless into the kitchen. He seemed about Sophie's age—early 20's—with black curly hair and a smooth-shaven face.

He bent to hug Sophie from behind. She leaned against him and reached back to wrap her arms around his waist.

"This is Guy," she said, rhyming it with "knee."

He smiled. "Hi."

"Hello."

"Annie is the American."

"Ah, yes. Are you coming tonight?"

"No," Annie said. She pressed her palms together and rested her cheek against them in pantomime. "Sleep."

"Tomorrow," said Sophie. "She promised. You can ride as many times as you want every day," she told Annie. "Kjartan takes the horses out all the time. You don't have to wait until tomorrow night if you don't want to."

"How late will you stay out tonight?" Annie asked.

Sophie tilted her head back to look at Guy. She pursed her mouth as she thought. "Maybe one o'clock?" she asked him. "One-thirty?"

"Probably."

"One-thirty," Annie repeated. "You ride all night?" She held up her hand to ward off the obvious answer. "I know it doesn't get dark, but still—how do you stay up so late?"

Sophie shrugged. "You don't feel tired. When it's light outside, you want to stay awake. You'll see."

"I have to say it's not helping me much right now." Annie's eyes burned with exhaustion. Her limbs felt heavy, her brain muddled. "I'm supposed to wait until tonight to go to sleep, but I'm so tired right now I can't imagine staying up another minute."

"You should sleep then," Guy advised.

"No, it'll just mess me up. You're supposed to stay up until your regular bedtime, or it'll take longer to get over jet lag."

Sophie clicked her tongue dismissively. "You're tired, you should sleep. Kjartan is right—soon you'll forget about time here. Go to bed. You'll feel better."

Even in her mental fog, Annie remembered the lock. "I forgot to ask about my door."

"You did ask," Sophie reminded her. "I'm sure Kjartan took care of it."

"When? Now?"

"Sure. Let's go see."

They retrieved their boots—Annie noticed both Sophie and Guy wore the slip on kind, a small detail that stirred Annie's imagination. She hadn't seen a French movie in some time—did all French people wear boots like that now? They left the house and ambled down the path toward the cottages.

Sophie and Guy led the way, holding hands and murmuring companionably. Annie stumbled along behind them, smiling to herself. A young woman that sweet deserved a boyfriend so obviously smitten with her.

Kjartan passed them on the path, carrying a small metal toolbox. "Fixed now," he said briefly without breaking his stride.

"Thank you," Annie called uncertainly. She turned to her escorts. Sophie and Guy stood gazing at each other with undisguised desire.

"Good," Sophie said, turning her attention to Annie. "Well, then, we'll leave you."

"You should go to sleep," Guy said. "I would." Annie caught the suggestive smile he directed at Sophie.

"I guess I will," Annie said. "I don't think I can stand up another minute."

"We'll see you later," said Sophie. She and Guy linked arms and turned toward their tent.

Annie had no doubt what would happen next. Somehow she couldn't picture them engaged in the foreign, mysterious passion of French lovers on a screen. Sophie seemed too comfortable in the world, too open-hearted to need the ploys Annie had watched French women use. Instead Annie imagined the two of them locked in love, eyes open, their mouths curved in knowing smiles, their lovemaking slow and generous. It wasn't envy Annie felt. Instead, in the same way young girls wish they could be horses, she wished she could be the two of them just once in her life.

With a tired sigh, she turned toward number 4, lusting only for sleep.

She took a quick shower before going to bed. She knew from the guidebook that most homes in Iceland were geothermically heated, but she didn't have a clear picture of what that meant. Standing in the shower, she saw her first evidence of it.

Two plastic tubes half the width of a garden hose snaked from the wall into the faucet handles. One tube was hot to the touch, even before she turned the handles. Coming from a desert climate, where every ounce of water mattered, Annie was used to restricting her showers to the time necessary to complete the job.

But here, on an island crisscrossed by rivers and bathed in rain almost every day, Annie let go of her inhibitions. She unleashed the naturally hot water and stood there as long as her tired body could stand it. She rinsed away the hours of travel, the stale air from two plane rides, the accumulated aches from sitting in confined spaces, and the last traces of American sweat. When she emerged from the shower, Annie felt as if she had taken her first real step toward surrender. For the next two and a half weeks, she would give herself completely to Iceland. She held on to that thought as she sank into sleep.

She awoke to the sun streaming through the curtains. Was it morning already? Had she slept all night?

She checked her watch. 8:00. AM or PM?

She knelt on her bed and parted the curtains. The ground above her cottage sloped upward toward the stable. She could just see the corner of the stable yard.

She saw Sophie and Guy and a few other people, all dressed in pants and boots and rain coats. She looked up. No rain. Back to the people.

Kjartan was there, dressed in dark pants, boots, and a long brown duster. He wore a wide-brimmed hat she imagined did well to keep the rain off his face. The other riders wore black riding caps buckled under the chin.

Hadn't Kjartan said the ride was at seven? They were late. Or maybe it was morning, and they were going out again. Annie's head felt no less foggy than before, although her body felt immeasurably improved by its rest. She needed coffee again— always, always. Maybe, she hoped, a pot was already brewed.

She took a moment to brush her teeth. The water from the sink tasted faintly of sulfur, just as the shower water had. Not surprising, she realized, considering the massive black mountain visible from the cottage. Iceland was dotted with volcanoes, most of them inactive, but every now and then one erupted, spewing ash and lava indiscriminately over town and country.

Annie ran a brush through her hair, then splashed water on

her face, hoping to draw out even a fraction of Sophie's fresh-scrubbed good looks.

She pulled from her bag a fresh pair of jeans. She had splurged in bringing two, along with sweatpants for relaxing around the cottage. She also brought rain pants and a rain coat. The rest of her bag was taken up by lesser necessities like under-wear, long johns, a bathing suit, one sweater, a few T-shirts, and socks.

Packing had been a strange pleasure this time. As part of her Freydis program, Annie challenged herself to travel light. She brought no make up, only moisturizer, sunscreen, and lip gloss. No perfume or jewelry or fancy shoes. She wore her hiking boots on the plane, and packed a pair of light-weight sneakers.

For now she slipped on a pair of clean jeans, a T-shirt, and her all-purpose red fleece coat. She sat on a stool near the door and pulled on her hiking boots. Stowing her key in her jacket pocket, she locked the door and pulled it closed behind her.

The riders were just moving out. Sophie and Guy saw Annie coming up the footpath and waved to her.

"Is it morning or night?" Annie called, only half joking.

"Night," Sophie answered. "Isn't it beautiful?" She turned to say something to Guy. He nodded and smiled. Again Annie noticed their easy companionship.

"Are you sure you won't come?" Sophie asked.

Annie was closer now, nearly at the horses. She shook her head. "Tomorrow."

The photos in the guidebook had been deceptive. Annie imagined the horses would be much smaller—almost pony-sized. But they were as large as any she'd seen, although stockier.

One thing the photos didn't lie about was the colors. Tan horses with long blond manes that wisped in the breeze. Dappled gray with salt and pepper tails. Blood-brown bays with inky black bangs hanging over their eyes.

Kjartan swept his leg over the saddle. He sat tall, his 6-foot-plus frame making the horse seem small again. He sat comfort-ably in the saddle, in complete command of the animal. He wore knee-high brown rubber boots with square heels that braced against the stirrups. His duster covered his thighs. Annie could see from where she was that it was actually a thick raincoat—much more substantial than the waterproof shell she had brought. His blond hair barely skiffed the nape of his neck below the brown leather hat.

Until he caught her eye, she didn't realize she'd been staring at him. She turned to observe the other riders. But still her eyes drifted back.

Just like the sagas. She felt as though she were sitting in a theater watching the opening credits begin to roll: This is Iceland. This is our hero. This is the saga of...which saga would she choose?

The name Kjartan was familiar to her. She had read the story of his ill-fated love for Gudrun—not a story she particularly liked. The guidebook claimed Gudrun was a revered heroine, but Annie couldn't imagine why.

Kjartan and Gudrun had been lovers in their youth, but then Kjartan went off to seek his fortune and, tired of waiting, Gudrun married his best friend. When Kjartan returned to Iceland, he had to settle for marrying another woman. Somehow Gudrun never forgave him for that. She stewed about it for years, then finally convinced her husband to kill his best friend. She didn't show any remorse until her deathbed, and even then it wasn't clear. When asked by her son which of the men in her life she had loved the most, Gudrun answered, "I loved him best whom I hurt the most." In Annie's eyes, that could only mean Kjartan. What kind of love story was that?

But they weren't just stories. The sagas were part history, part legend. The Kjartan she saw before her could be a descendent of any one of the Vikings she read about. Looking at him, Annie felt an unexpected awe. It was as though she were seeing in the flesh a descendant of Achilles. It was more than his name. Annie noticed when she paged through the airport phone book that many names came straight from the sagas—Olaf, Gudrun, Gudrid, Thorsten, other Kjartans. No, it was the way he looked, the way he moved with a quiet strength that hinted at much greater power in reserve. She had no difficulty imagining this Kjartan playing the part of a saga hero.

He caught her staring at him again. Annie jerked her eyes away.

Kjartan nodded to her. "Good night."

"'Night." She was sure her cheeks were as red as her coat.

She stepped back further than necessary to let the horses and their riders pass by. She needed distance. The place was already working on her, teasing her notions of time, putting flesh to the images she had seen on screen and in books.

She turned back toward the cottage. She was halfway down the path when she remembered her craving for coffee. No matter how good it sounded at the moment, she decided to wait until morning. This way she might be able to sleep again in a few hours, and wake tomorrow feeling normal.

If such a thing were even possible there.

Kjartan cursed himself for even thinking it.

But damn, she was pretty.

His eyes kept coming back to her: standing there with her hands stuffed in the pockets of her red coat, the wind blowing her dark hair against her face, cheeks rosy from the cold.

When he saw her standing in his office that afternoon he had to take a moment to catch his breath. Why should that be? She was no one to him, just another stranger passing through his house. He saw enough of them every day during the summer to catalog a whole range of females—the shy, the glamorous, the shrill.

He had to admit to the easy confidence of American women. They seemed to approach the world from such a different perspective. They expected a certain openness from people that Kjartan had never understood. Why should strangers ask each other such personal questions—where were you born, what is your job, are you married? Annie hadn't asked him any of that, but seeing her in his office, then sipping coffee in his kitchen, he felt...dread. A traveler alone searched for companions. Hadn't she already found Sophie? It was only a matter of time before she attached herself to Kjartan and asked him to open his life for her inspection.

She had no right.

He caught her looking at him, studying him. Why should that make him feel so exposed? But it did—her bright eyes taking it all in, drawing him to look at her when what he should have done was look away.

But she was pretty—he had to admit that much. Her face was delicate, with high round cheekbones and a slim, freckled nose. She wasn't too thin, the way some women allowed themselves to be. He sometimes looked at them and wondered how they kept from blowing over in the wind. They were the women who whined about the cold, whose faces grew slack with dejection when they realized they couldn't automatically ride well just because they wanted to, who demanded some relief with a six-hour ride only half over—what could he do, have them heli-coptered away? But Annie seemed sturdy enough. He was curious to know how she would handle the horses.

He had watched her in his rear view mirror, watched her eyes blink heavily and finally close, her body slump against the window. He slowed the van as he pulled into the drive of his house, not wanting to wake her. He turned off the motor and turned to look at her. He stayed that way for a minute longer than he should have, but no one was near, and he was curious.

Why was a woman like that traveling alone? Where was her boyfriend, her husband, a lover? And why Iceland? Kjartan was used to Europeans coming over on a whim, but what compelled this woman to make plans on a Sunday and arrive three days later? That spoke of a boldness he hadn't seen in many women. Maybe it was that strange American confidence that made Annie Linley think she could come here and get along, just because she wanted it that way.

Carrying her single, small bag to cottage number 4 Kjartan had wondered even further: Why so light? Why so simple? When had he ever seen a woman travel with less than half her wardrobe?

He felt a burn in his stomach. He thought of Marta's clothes, laid out in piles on the bed.

"You're only going for a month," he had teased her. "You'll have to change clothes three times a day to wear all this."

"I don't know what the weather will be like," Marta had answered. "I don't want to have to buy things there."

Kjartan had left her to her packing and gone back downstairs. He still wondered whether that was a mistake. If he had stayed in their bedroom, asked her more questions, allowed her the time to talk, would she have told him? Had she even decided by then, or did the idea only come to her once she was in California?

Kjartan left Annie's bag at the door of the cottage and walked back to his own house to find a key. He approached the van with light steps, not exactly tip-toeing—what would people make of that?—but keeping his boots from scuffing the gravel. He eased open the driver-side door rather than risk waking her with the sound of the sliding panel. He leaned in and laid the key beside her.

She looked so uncomfortable, braced by the strap, her head leaning to one side. Kjartan knelt on the front seat and reached behind to snap open the latch on her seatbelt. She stirred slightly, and he pulled his hand back. With a gentle pucker of her lips she sighed then and lay down on the seat. Kjartan took a moment longer to gaze at her. Her blunt brown hair fell in a silk wave across her cheek. She rested her hands beneath her face, like a cherub.

Where was her man?

Who had let her get away?

And why should that matter to him?

3

With coffee out of the question, Annie turned her attention to a more compelling matter: food.

It was a shared joke with Shannon that every time their two families got together the earth sank another few feet. Food seemed to be constantly on their minds. That habit carried through to Annie and Shannon's adult years. Every time the cousins met they ate their way from one end of the city to the other—Mexican restaurants, German, Italian.

Except this time. Annie had arrived at the Minneapolis airport a little after 5:00 PM, and left for Iceland just a few hours later. She and Shannon only had time for a quick, expensive bite in the airport. Annie had eaten a second dinner halfway through her flight over, but those calories were long since gone. She craved crunch: apple, carrot, anything. She also needed a stout helping of bread.

The farm's website promised three meals a day. Annie's cottage contained a small kitchen, but she had no supplies. She would have to find a store the next day, but for now she would have to make do with whatever she could find.

She rang the doorbell to the house. She waited a respectable amount of time, then walked in.

"Hello?"

"Hello?" a woman called from the kitchen.

Annie unlaced her hiking boots and left them with several

other pairs of boots clustered near the door. She padded into the kitchen.

"Hello," said a woman sitting alone at the table, sipping a cup of coffee. Annie guessed she was in her 60's. Her gray hair was shortly-cropped, and she wore loose black pants and a ratty blue sweater. "Have you just arrived?" She sounded German, Annie thought, or maybe Austrian.

"Yes. This morning."

"Have you been here before?"

"No, I—"

"You're the American?"

"Yes."

"Have you met Kjartan?"

"Yes."

The questions came so quickly, Annie barely had time to consider her answers.

"Isn't it beautiful here? Have you seen the horses?"

The woman's voice was just a tad too loud, and crackly—maybe a smoker. She wore small round glasses that emphasized the moon shape of her face. Her mouth was wide and perpetually in motion.

But it was her teeth that Annie found most interesting. They were the largest teeth she had ever seen. Each appeared perfectly square, with wide spaces between them, giving the impression that the woman had to make do with half as many teeth as the normal allotment, while still filling her whole mouth. They looked like tiles missing their grout.

The woman paused, waiting for Annie's answer.

"I'm sorry?" Annie said, ashamed to be caught staring.

"The horses!" the woman crackled.

"Yes, they're—"

"Why are you here?"

"Well," Annie laughed, the woman's friendly aggression finally getting to her, "that was direct."

"I can be more direct," the woman answered, smiling good-naturedly. "I've been waiting here since two hours for you to come to dinner so I can talk to you. I almost had to wake you up."

Still chuckling, Annie asked, "Who are you?"

"Etta. I'm here for a visit like you. You need something to eat."

"Yes, I do." The rapid conversation had used up whatever calories Annie had left from her last meal. "I'm An—"

"Annie. Yes, I know all about you. Will toast satisfy you? Or do you need fish? What did you eat today?"

"Um, fish might be good."

Etta bounded from the table and set about opening cupboards, drawers, the refrigerator. "It was greasy tonight, but not bad. Here, start on this." She thrust a basket at Annie and went back to foraging.

Annie lifted the red cloth napkin covering the basket and tore off a chunk of the thick white bread inside. "How did you know about me?"

"I ask Kjartan every day who's coming. It's good here, but I am bored with the same guests. There are other Germans in the two cottages close to you—very boring people. Thank God I found Sophie and Guy. They camped at the school and I said—" She pointed her finger in emphasis. "'No, you must stay here.' I made my husband load their tent in our car before they could change their minds. Have you met Sophie? Was I right to make her come?"

"She's lovely," Annie agreed.

"And so smart. Do you know she will be a doctor?"

"No," Annie said, readjusting her impression of the young woman, "I didn't know that."

"What are you?" Etta asked.

"Um, a teacher."

"A teacher? Good. You should talk to Kjartan. The school here is looking for someone. Can you teach all ages?"

"I already have a job."

"You should leave it. Try something new. Wouldn't you like to live someplace like this?"

"No," Annie said with a laugh. "I don't think so."

"Why not?"

"I don't know, it's just not... What a strange question."

"Are you married?"

"No."

"Why?" Etta asked. "You're pretty. Are you terrible to live with?"

"I don't think so."

Etta pulled a plate of warmed fish from the microwave and set it in front of Annie. "I tell you why I ask," Etta said. "I'm looking for a wife for Kjartan."

Annie coughed. "Does he know that?"

"Yes. Of course he hates me for it, but what can he do? I pay, so he must suffer with me."

"How long have you been here?"

Etta plopped back onto her chair. "This time? Already twenty-six days. In my life? Twelve years."

"Wow."

"My husband and I come here every summer. We came before Kjartan owned the farm—when his wife's parents owned it."

"His wife? I thought you said—"

"No," Etta waved her hand, "she left. It's just Kjartan now. And Petra in the summers to help with the tourists."

"Petra."

Etta groaned as she stood. Annie couldn't tell if it was in response to the name or because of creaky joints. Etta carried her cup to the coffee pot.

"Oh," Annie said, forgetting her vow to wait, "I'd love some of that."

"It's old—I made it two hours ago. I'll make fresh."

"No, don't bother—"

But Etta had already poured it down the drain.

"Who's Petra?" Annie asked.

"Another German—that's all I see here. Now you know why I almost had to wake you." Etta scooped out coffee from the canister. "The only other Americans I've seen in Iceland are on the tour buses. They get to town, get off the bus, take pictures, get back on. Why aren't you on a tour?"

"I don't know. It's not my thing."

"You're adventurous."

Annie laughed. "I don't know about that." She pretended to dismiss Etta's assessment, but inwardly it pleased her.

"Petra," Etta said, picking up the dangling thread of their conversation, "has worked here for five summers—almost since Marta left." Seeing Annie's quizzical look, Etta added, "Marta was his wife. Ran off to California. Petra came over on holiday to work with the horses. She thinks she will marry Kjartan one of these times."

"Will she?"

Etta scoffed. "No. Not her."

"Why not?" Annie had been so absorbed she had neglected the fish. Now she flaked it apart with her fork, cutting into the bread crumb crust, and speared a bite. "Mmm."

"Excellent, isn't it?" Etta asked. "That fish was swimming three hours ago. Wilhelm caught it himself."

"Wilhelm?"

"My husband, but you won't see him. Fish, sleep, fish, sleep—that's all he does. Have you been to the pool yet?"

Annie's brain scurried to change direction. "The pool. No."

Etta stood and pulled a coffee cup from the cupboard. "Milk? Sugar?"

"Milk, please."

Etta poured herself another cup and set both on the table. "You should go to the pool tonight. It closes, but the back door is unlocked."

"Not tonight," Annie said. "I'll go tomorrow."

Annie took a sip of the dark, muddy brew. Apparently Etta believed in using the same proportions as Sophie did, because this cup was no less assaultive than the one Annie had tasted that afternoon.

Etta asked, "Do you know why the children here are so healthy?"

Annie found herself enjoying the pace of their conversation. It was like watching images flash on a screen, each one there for only a blink, so that she barely had time to register what she had seen. She gave in to Etta's mad, structureless discourse, curious to see where it would lead them next.

"No, why are they so healthy?"

"Because of the pool. It has natural minerals in it. You'll think it's dirty, but it's the minerals."

"I'll try it tomorrow."

Etta paused long enough to take a sip. Then she dove back in. "And of course you know about the sagas."

"I've read some of them."

"I've read all of them. Wonderful, aren't they?"

"Yes, I—"

"Have you read *Laxdaela Saga*? The one about Kjartan and Gudrun?"

"Yes."

"That's a terrible story, don't you think?"

"Yes, I do."

"Do you know people call that a love story?"

"I don't see why," Annie said. "She had him killed."

"Yes, but on her deathbed she says," Etta cleared her crackly throat, "'I loved him best whom I treated the worst.' People think that's romantic. They think Gudrun was a woman to admire."

Annie shrugged. "I think she's awful."

Etta pursed her lips and nodded in satisfaction. She took another sip and peered at Annie critically. "You came alone. Why?"

Annie considered telling this strange woman the truth—all of it. Instead she settled for half a truth. "I wanted to make myself strong."

Etta grinned. She slapped her hand against Annie's. "See? I knew you would be interesting. I should have woken you earlier."

THE RIDERS RETURNED past 1:00. Annie saw them trotting up the path in the almost dusky light.

"Does it get dark at all?" she asked Etta.

"A little bit more each night. Maybe for an hour or two now."

Kjartan rode at the rear. Several of the riders slumped in their saddles, clearly worn out from the night-long ride, but Kjartan sat tall, his posture easy, casual. He barely seemed to move as his horse glided up the trail.

Annie returned to one of Etta's earlier subjects. "Why are you looking for a wife for him? He shouldn't have any problem finding one himself."

"If he wanted one," Etta agreed. "He doesn't believe me when I tell him he needs one. I tell him he's getting old and angry. He's only thirty-eight and acts eighty. He says having another wife will make it worse."

Etta laughed. It was the first time she had laughed all night, and it made Annie smile suspiciously.

"What's so funny?"

"I am a smart woman," Etta answered.

"Yes...?"

Etta patted Annie's hand and stood. "Good night."

Puzzled, Annie turned to watch Etta disappear down the hall. Soon she heard the door open and close. The woman was gone.

Annie carried the dishes to the sink. She considered leaving them there, then thought better of it. If the policy of the house was that guests served themselves whenever they wished, they were probably expected to clean as well. Annie rinsed her fork, the cups, and the plate and loaded them into the dishwasher.

With the water running, she didn't hear him come in. He stood in the doorway of the kitchen and said, "You're still awake."

Startled, Annie turned. There was something incongruous about seeing a man otherwise fully-dressed for the outdoors, but wearing only socks. Kjartan removed his hat. His thick yellowish-brown hair was matted with either sweat or rain. Annie noticed blond stubble on his face, a light scar just above his right eyebrow. For a moment she took all this in, unable after so full an evening of talking to form even a mundane sentence.

Kjartan dipped his head and moved through the kitchen toward his office. Unconsciously, Annie took a step back, the same way she had with the horses.

"Did you have a good ride?" she managed.

"*Já.*"

Again the sound confused her. "Oh, why not?"

There was a brief moment of silence.

"Yes," he corrected. "It was good."

Annie rolled her eyes at herself. "Good," she repeated, nodding stupidly. She was grateful he couldn't see her from his office. Why was she suddenly acting so stupid—so awkward? She realized it was because she knew too much about him, and felt guilty for it.

"Well, good night," she called.

Kjartan stepped out of his office, back into the doorway of the kitchen. He nodded to her politely. "Okay, good night."

Annie turned and walked stiffly down the hall. She quickly pulled on her boots, leaving the laces untied for the sake of speed. As she reached for her jacket she glanced down the hall, paranoid that he might see her fumbling retreat. But the hallway was empty. She opened the door and escaped.

Kjartan wandered slowly into his living room. It was his favorite room during the summer, though he rarely had time to enjoy it. A wide span of windows looked out over his pastures. He could watch the horses graze, the colts burst into sudden leaps, the stallion chase down a recalcitrant mare.

He could also see the summer cottages.

Kjartan watched Annie walk across the foot path, her hair swinging against the collar of her jacket. He wondered at finding her there alone in his house at that time of night. Had she been waiting for him?

Of course not, he thought. Why would she? If she needed something she would have asked.

Then why was she there?

He still had work to do. He had left Petra to supervise the riders while they unsaddled their horses and brushed them down. Meanwhile Kjartan booted up the computer to check for any late messages. He knew he had at least three people coming for an 8:00 ride the next morning—no, this morning already, he corrected himself—and he wanted to make sure they were the only ones. He would take them out while Petra tended to some of the other, seemingly endless chores associated with the farm and the horses.

There was an e-mail from a hotel booking a night ride for three of their guests. Kjartan pressed his fingers against his closed eyelids. Summers were good money, but so much work.

Still, even a hard day there was better than any day he'd had in the city. He printed the message and shut down the computer.

His mind shifted into automatic. He returned to the stable, said his final goodnights to Sophie and Guy, gave Petra her assignment for the morning, dismissed her for the night. He waited while the three of them parted, Sophie and Guy holding hands as they walked toward their tent, Petra turning to enter the house.

Kjartan watched the two young lovers amble away. They were so easy together, never fighting that he saw, constantly affectionate in so many small, tender ways. Of course, he thought —this was their holiday. There was nothing real to spoil their good time. Still, he wondered if what he saw was what they were, whether in Iceland or back at home. In a way, he hoped so, the way he knew the colts kicked up their heels even when he wasn't watching them. He wanted to believe that somewhere people were enjoying love, even if he weren't a part of it.

Kjartan turned from the melancholy gray of the landscape back toward the lights of the stable. He went in, calling the horses by name, ready to inspect them before turning them loose.

He paused to stroke the jaw of the horse he had ridden. Wearily he leaned against the horse's neck.

Was she waiting for me? Kjartan wondered. He whispered the question to his horse. *Var hun ad bida eftir mer?* The gelding offered no opinion.

A GOOD TRICK, Annie thought, lying sleepless in her bed. Etta knew exactly what would happen. She wanted Annie and Kjartan to be alone.

Now she was glad she hadn't told Etta the whole reason why she was there.

To live like a heroine from the sagas, she imagined saying.

"Good!" Etta would have answered. "Here's your Kjartan."

4

Annie awoke to a knock at her door. She took a minute to gather her senses: I'm here. In Iceland. In someone else's house.

Rather than take the time to put on a bra, she slipped her jacket over her sleep shirt before opening the door.

A tall redhead in knee-high rubber boots stood on the porch.

"Annie?"

"Yes."

"Kjartan told me to wake you at 9:00. He said not to miss breakfast."

Annie processed the information slowly. "Okay..."

"The school has breakfast only until 10:00."

Another German, Annie realized. Etta was right—they were everywhere there.

"Okay," Annie repeated. "What should I do?"

"I came back for you. I can drive you there."

"Ten minutes?" Annie asked.

"No problem."

The woman descended the cottage steps and strode off toward the house.

Annie took off her jacket and wandered into the bathroom. She surveyed her face in the mirror.

Something was already different, she decided. She was here now—it wasn't just an idea or a plan, she was actually here. She had moved beyond her fear and done something extraordinary. Already her Freydis program—her deliberate attempt to become bolder—was working. Annie smiled and praised her reflection. "Good job."

In the driveway the redhead leaned against a white compact car. "Ready?"

Annie nodded and got in. The car was jammed with papers, food wrappers, clothes, a horse blanket, and several pairs of shoes. An open bag of potato chips rested near the gear shift. A plastic mug of coffee balancing on the dashboard steamed the windshield above it.

The woman jerked the car to life and jetted to the edge of the driveway.

"Are you Petra?" Annie guessed.

"Yes. I'm sorry, I should have introduced myself." Petra shifted the car into park and offered her hand. Her grip was dry and stiff. That formality over, she plunged back into drive and spun from the gravel to the asphalt. She didn't appear to look either way before committing to her charge.

Instinctively Annie braced against her seat and checked her side mirror for any car they might have cut off. She saw none. In fact, turning now to look at the miles of flat roadway stretching behind them, she saw not a single car anywhere. No wonder Petra could afford to drive like that.

In less than a minute—what would probably have been only a ten-minute walk—Petra whipped into the parking lot of a single-story white concrete building. Two other, smaller buildings shared the same lot. On the side of one, painted in red letters, was the word "*sundlaug,*" and an arrow pointing to the right. Annie noticed steam rising from fenced area just beyond the building.

"Is that the pool?" she asked.

"Yes. The cafeteria is here." Petra pointed to the main building. She exited the car, leaving Annie to follow.

Annie couldn't tell if the woman was shy or hostile. Thinking of Etta's peculiar social skills, Annie decided to give Petra the benefit of the doubt.

Annie followed through the open double doors of the school.

Shoes and coats crammed the entryway. Annie bent to unlace her hiking boots and add them to the collection. She searched for somewhere to hang her jacket. Every wall peg was taken, each bearing not just one coat, but several.

The cafeteria was the size of an American classroom, with space for just five long dining tables and a separate serving table set flush against the wall. She could see the kitchen just beyond. Petra and another woman stood at the sink washing pots.

Based on the amount of clothing in the entryway, Annie expected to see a horde of people in the cafeteria. Instead, the only diners were Sophie, Guy, Etta, and a man with shoulder-length white hair.

Sophie stood and greeted her with a kiss on the cheek. "We slept late, too."

"Where are all the people?" Annie asked her.

"People?"

"That go with all the shoes and coats."

Etta answered for her. "Tourist groups," she said. "Mostly students. They rent the school to sleep here and have breakfast. Then they get back on their buses to visit every hot springs so the girls can show off in their bikinis."

"Who would want to see something like that?" scoffed the white-haired gentleman beside her. He stood and offered Annie his hand. "Hello, I'm Wilhelm." He pronounced the "w" as a soft "v." He wore a broad smile that Annie soon discovered was his perpetual expression.

"Did my wife counsel you last night?" he asked.

"Counsel me?"

"Did she solve your life?"

"It doesn't need solving," Annie answered with a smile of her own. She liked to hear how people less familiar with English assembled its words and phrases to suit their meaning. Over the years she had tutored students whose first language was Spanish, and had watched them labor to make sense of the irrational nuances of English grammar. She felt the same frustration over the romance languages' designation of nouns as either feminine or masculine. She wondered how people remembered the sex of a toaster, an umbrella, an argument, the rain.

"I told her she should move here and teach at the school," Etta announced to the group.

Sophie nodded thoughtfully. "Yes, that would be good. Unless you don't like the cold?"

"No," Annie answered emphatically.

"Oh, then maybe not so good," said Sophie. "Sorry, Etta, you will have to find someone else." Sophie's eyes sparkled mischievously. Annie wondered if this was a conversation she and Etta had had before.

"How many more teachers will come here this summer?" Etta complained. "I told Kjartan I'm not leaving until I find one. This poor little school..." She turned to her husband. "We're not leaving."

"Good," he answered, grinning at Annie. "Why would we leave?"

"Are you enjoying your vacation?" Annie asked.

"Yes," Wilhelm answered, "but it is always too short."

"Five weeks is infinity," Etta said.

"She complains, but she would never let me come alone."

"How would you know if I'm here or not? Unless I swam in the river..."

Wilhelm grinned at Annie. "It is very good fishing here."

Etta rolled her eyes. "I told you. Fish, sleep, fish."

"Would you like to go fishing today?" Wilhelm offered. "I can show you where they're good."

"Uh..." Annie looked to Sophie for assistance.

"You might like it," Sophie said. "But first, when will you go riding?"

"I don't know. What are my choices?"

"You should go tonight," answered Sophie. "We're going at noon also, but it will be a short ride. You would like where we're going tonight."

"But maybe a short ride would be better, since it's my first time."

"No, you go tonight," Sophie pressed. "You will learn more if you have more time. I want to make a rider out of you. A short trip will not be enough."

Annie considered the advice. "How many people will go?"

Sophie looked to Guy. "How many, do you think?"

"Mm, maybe six, seven—eight with Annie."

"We're taking the van, so it can't be many more," Sophie explained.

"Taking the van where?"

"To where we left the horses early in the week. Tonight we make the trip in reverse. That's how I know you will like it."

Satisfied that Sophie had her best interests at heart, Annie agreed to the plan. They made arrangements to meet for an early dinner at the house before leaving around 6:00.

"I'll probably see you before then," Sophie said. "Maybe at the pool?"

"I don't know. Maybe. I want to look around today. I don't really know what I'm doing yet."

"You should go fishing," Wilhelm insisted.

"Maybe. Let me eat something first. Then I can think."

Sophie and Guy said their goodbyes.

Annie searched for her first cup of coffee. An industrial-sized coffee urn dispensed more of the dark, bitter blend. Annie resolved to learn to love it. She was here now, and would experience all of it, never backing away from anything simply because it was out of her normal range.

If Freydis could drink coffee this harsh, Annie thought, so could she—assuming, that was, the Icelanders had coffee a thousand years ago.

A serving table sat flush against the wall opposite the dining tables. Annie scanned the selection: lunch meats, cheeses, a soft white creamy substance that looked like yogurt. Corn flakes and an oat, seed, and raisin mixture which she took to be muesli, something she had heard of but never tried. Wheat bread, black bread, apricot and strawberry jams. Two bowls of pickled fish.

Seeing her stand there lost, Wilhelm said, "Try this."

She watched while he fixed himself a plate. He toasted a slice of wheat bread, then spread on a thin layer of butter. Next he laid on a slice of Swiss cheese, and finally spread over the cheese a spoonful of apricot jam.

Annie had never considered cheese and jam together, but why not? She duplicated the concoction, then searched for other adventures in dining. She spooned some of the yogurt into a bowl, and helped herself to a glass of boxed juice. Although the picture on the side was of an orange, the liquid that came out looked more like colored water than pulpy juice. So what? she mused. Try it.

With Sophie and Guy gone, Annie had all of Etta's attention.

"What happened last night?" she asked without subtlety.

Annie eyed her sternly. "Nothing."

Etta turned to her husband. "Don't you think she's pretty?"

"Yes, with nice green eyes," he answered, as though assessing the merits of a trout. His smile still in place, Wilhelm asked, "Does she try to match you to Kjartan?"

"Yes," Annie groaned. Already she felt a solidarity with Wilhelm. She took a bite of the toast and nodded approvingly. "Delicious."

"Try that," Etta said, pointing to the yogurt-like cream. "It's *skyr*. Have you heard of that? Famous in Iceland."

The *skyr* tasted sweeter than yogurt, but had a tart aftertaste, almost like sour cream with sugar added. Wilhelm went back to the serving table and returned with a bowl of strawberries in syrup. "Try this," he said, dumping them into the *skyr*.

Annie stirred them and tasted again. She was sure she blushed.

How could these people know what was happening to her? As a little girl, Annie had taken the same lunch to school every single day: peanut butter and jelly. As an adult, she had a range of four restaurants she frequented, all within three miles of her home. She could order without looking at the menus, because once she found a dish she liked she ordered the same thing every time. She didn't want to try anything else and risk being disappointed.

In a life that had often shifted before Annie could brace herself for it, she learned to depend on the safety of routine. In times of family crisis, it was the drudgery of sameness that kept her from spinning into despair. Even if the only things she could control in a day were whether she brushed her hair or her teeth first, which foot got the first sock, which cereal she pulled from the cupboard, the order in which she read the comics... Her routines kept her tethered to earth. She proved she could count on herself. Others might change, might shock, might pull the floor out from beneath her, but she knew she was always the same.

But here, on an island just a whisper below the Arctic Circle, far from her family and friends, free of the burden of predictability, Annie could be someone else—wanted to be, craved being—someone else. She had sat in the library—when? Only a few days ago?—reading the sagas about men and women for whom life must have changed every hour. Yet they persevered. More than that, they grew stronger. They lived a full life, no matter how short or filled with pain. They loved hard and hated fiercely, and drew from the place a passion Annie had never found in her own life.

All that from a taste of jam over cheese, Annie thought. From strawberries and *skyr*.

Get a grip.

But it was more than that, and she knew it. She was already changing. Her task, as she saw it, was to make sure she didn't back away from it. This was her chance to fill out the edges of her life, if only for a few weeks. If she failed—shied away from it, or fell back into her old ways—she would go home hurting worse than when she had come. She was sure of it.

A long post-breakfast walk in the damp, cold air reinforced Annie's belief that she had crossed over some invisible barrier and now stood in the world of her future. She didn't feel like herself. Part of it, she reasoned, was the effect of chilled rain on her face. It was July, a month in which she would normally be rushing from air conditioned house to air conditioned car before the searing heat could attack her. During the summers Annie kept to a daily routine of rising with the sun at 4:30 so she could walk in the cool of the morning. By 9:00 the heat would wilt even those who were used to it. That was the time for errands such as grocery shopping or browsing in the book store.

By late morning she liked to be settled in her favorite chair with her second cup of coffee and whatever novel she was reading that week. She made a list at the beginning of each summer of all the classics she needed to revisit: works by Dostoevsky, Milton, George Eliot, Jane Austen. Since May she had re-read four Shakespeare comedies, a collection of Browning's poems, and a fair rendition of Chaucer, translated from the Middle English. In between she treated herself to modern novels and true-life adventures, usually focusing on Arctic exploration —a landscape that had always fascinated a girl who grew up in the desert.

But now, walking down a strange road, the hood of her rain-coat cinched around her face, Annie had no plan in mind. She had no place to be, nothing to accomplish this hour or the one after that.

She felt a little giddy.

She had refused Wilhelm's repeated offers to take her fishing. She wanted to experience the place alone. She wanted to form her own impressions, see things through her own eyes rather than those of someone more experienced.

She wanted, she realized, to let Iceland touch her. She wanted to open up to it and not guess what might happen next.

As she strolled down the roadside trail she had seen the riders come up the night before—or really, Annie reminded herself, that morning—she took in the spaciousness of the view. She could see as far as the rainy mist allowed—out across the pastures to a small lake, up toward the black mountain rising above the road, back toward the farmhouse, its red steel roof shining in the wet. She listened to her feet crunch the loose rock. Smelled the damp hay, the fresh manure, the wet ground. She buried her fingers in the pockets of her coat, relishing the cold sting on their tips. What might pass for a typical—even beautiful, for all she knew—summer day in Iceland was like a February day in Tucson. How could that be? How could she have been in one world just days before, and find herself here this morning, wet and cold and happy?

She paused at the fence to look at the horses. About a dozen of them lay near what appeared to be a stone trough.

From a distance, it was the blond-maned horses that captured her attention. They reminded her of California beach girls, with their reddish tans and sun-bleached hair. Standing near the group was a black horse, his long black mane whipping in the wind. He stared at the road—or maybe, Annie thought, at her—and from the way he held his head, the way he jutted his chest forward and stood braced against the grass, Annie could see the stallion knew he was beautiful. She imagined him a man, hands on his hips, red cape snapping in the wind.

Smiling at her own foolishness, Annie ducked her head back into the rain and kept moving.

She saw Wilhelm standing riverside across the road. He waved and returned to his work. Annie was certain she had made the right choice between fishing in the rain and strolling in it. Besides, Wilhelm would have wanted her to talk, and right now it was the last thing Annie wanted. She needed the quiet to collect her heart. She could feel it expanding with each passing hour, and needed time to build a new structure to support it.

Eyes down, shielded from the wind, ears muffled by her tightly-drawn hood, Annie didn't sense the riders until they were almost to her. When she looked up they were only a few paces away, and trotting quickly toward her. Frightened, she crossed to the other side of the road.

Even with his head down, face hidden by the wide brim of his hat, Kjartan was unmistakable. He rode differently from the rest of them—tall, relaxed in the saddle, arms loose, gloved hands holding the reins as though they were delicate stems. He didn't look up as he passed her, but pressed forward, driving the party home. Annie searched for familiar faces, but realized Sophie and Guy would not be in this group—they were going out later. Annie wondered how many groups Kjartan guided every day. If this day were any indication, it was at least three. Home at 1:00 in the morning, out again before 9:00, then noon again, then another night ride. Hours every day spent in the saddle. She admired his stamina.

KJARTAN PASSED before realizing she was there. He rode by rote, letting the horse pick its course and pace. His mind was on the next group he had to lead, on the supplies he needed to buy, on the list of chores that grew ever longer as the summer progressed. He tried not to think of himself—of the accumulated exhaustion he kept at bay by never stopping, of the emptiness he knew might overtake him if he didn't keep running. Sometimes it was better not to think. Better just to do.

Suddenly there was movement in front of them, the flash of a blue raincoat, and there was Annie watching from across the street. He barely caught sight of her before he passed. What was the point in looking? She was just another tourist, here for a brief adventure, then home again to whatever her life was.

He wondered what impulse compelled him to dismount that morning and go back inside the stable while the tourist riders waited for him. In as casual a tone as he could muster, he had told Petra to wake Annie in time for breakfast. When had he ever done that before? His guests could look after themselves. He exited the stable shaking his head at himself, while at same time feeling satisfied he had done the right thing.

Maybe, Kjartan thought now, pressing on through the rain, it was that same sense of protectiveness that made him check on the horses several times during the night whenever a blizzard blew. Annie was alone, and no matter how competent she might be at taking care of herself in America, she was in Iceland now. A good host reaches out to his guests to see that they're comfortable.

That's all it is, Kjartan decided. Anyone would do the same.

5

The riders clustered in the stable yard while Kjartan and Petra loaded two horses into the trailer.

"I thought you said the horses were already where we're going," Annie said.

"These are the horses Kjartan and Petra will ride. They always bring their own."

"Who are these other people?" Annie mumbled.

Sophie nodded toward a dapper, gray-bearded man and his much-younger companion. "Those two are staying in one of the cottages."

The Germans Etta had mentioned, Annie thought.

"And that girl and her parents are from Sweden, I think."

"Are they staying here?"

"No. They came only for the ride. And that man in the black boots works in the stable. He'll drive the van back here."

Kjartan called for them to load the van. Annie sat in the back next to the stable hand. She noticed she was the only one paranoid enough to be wearing her riding helmet already. She unbuckled it and slipped it onto her lap.

They drove forty minutes down a paved two-lane road, then turned onto a dirt track. Farmhouses clustered to create a small village on the edge of the sea. Sophie pointed to one of the pastures where a small herd of horses grazed. "Those are ours."

The van pulled beside the pasture. The stable hand moved

into the driver's seat, waited for Kjartan to unload the horses, then pulled back onto the road.

I'm stuck, Annie thought. No turning back.

"That one is my favorite," Sophie said, pointing to a light gray horse with a salt and pepper mane. "He likes to go fast, but he will listen to me." She whispered conspiratorially, "Let's go stand by him so I can get him."

Sophie scanned the rest of the herd. "You should ask for that one, the brown mare with a silver mane. Guy rode her as we came here last time. He said she was very good."

Petra approached with a bay gelding in tow. "This one is yours," she told Annie.

Annie searched for the mare Sophie had identified. The Swedish teenager was already saddling her.

"Are you sure?" Annie asked, looking to Sophie for support. "Is this one good for beginners?"

Petra handed Annie the reins. "Kjartan says this is yours."

Sophie showed Annie how to saddle the horse. She fastened one strap tightly against the horse's belly, and drew another up under his tail. "Would you like help getting on?" Sophie asked, bending to offer her hands. She hoisted Annie into the saddle, then adjusted the length of her stirrups.

Annie noticed that all the other riders seemed able to do these things for themselves. For now, she was more than content to let Sophie show her everything, since neither Petra nor Kjartan seemed interested in the task.

Kjartan waited on horseback for the other riders to mount, then nosed his horse down the trail. The other riders quickly fell into line. Following Sophie's advice, Annie waited for everyone to pass before bringing up the rear.

But her horse had other ideas.

Not content to watch the swaying backsides of his companions, Annie's gelding trotted up the sideline until he was at the head of the pack. Pulling back on the reins did nothing to dissuade him. He continued his rapid course, while Annie's heart thundered in panic.

She turned back to look for Sophie, and was grateful to see her already hurrying up to the front.

"This horse likes to be first," Sophie confirmed. "You should tell Kjartan you don't want him."

The horse continued its teeth-jarring trot.

"But he said this horse was good for beginners."

"Do you want to be in front?" Sophie asked.

"No!" There was nothing Annie wanted less.

"Then you should tell him—now, before we start for the cliffs."

The word "cliffs" brought a desperate chill to Annie's heart. She turned again, this time searching for Kjartan. She was grateful when Sophie called to him.

Kjartan joined them at the front of the line. "Something wrong?"

"Yes," Annie answered, looking to Sophie for support. "I'm afraid of this horse." She hated to admit it, but she hated even more the idea that her wild ride might continue. "Sophie says this horse likes to be in front—I don't. I want to be in back. I don't like to go fast."

Kjartan accepted the complaint without comment. He pulled a tether from the pocket of his duster and clipped it to his horse's bridle. He leaned over and clipped the other end to the bridle on Annie's horse.

"Go ahead," Kjartan told Sophie. He shouted over his shoulder, "Petra! Come lead."

Annie could feel his annoyance. "I'm really sorry—"

He answered gruffly, "No need." As Petra passed him they spoke briefly in Icelandic. Petra nodded and hurried to overtake Sophie, whose horse was now a good distance ahead. "Have to keep together," Kjartan mumbled in English.

"Sure," Annie said. "Sorry for the trouble."

They waited in silence for the other riders to pass. Then Kjartan urged his horse forward. Annie's horse followed obediently at his side.

Kjartan held his reins with one hand and rested the other hand on his thigh. He looked comfortable, relaxed, despite the stern set of his mouth. Annie gripped the reins in both hands, the way she remembered Shannon showing her years before. She sat stiff, nervous, embarrassed. So much for blending in. So much for her big, bold adventure. She felt like a child harnessed to a grown up.

Six hours like this, Annie thought. Great. What was I thinking?

I thought I could be someone else.

Kjartan stared ahead, apparently content to ride in silence. Annie withdrew into her own protective shell. If Kjartan wanted to ignore her, that was fine—in fact, she preferred it. She had already suffered enough attention for one night.

I don't like to go fast, she'd told Kjartan.

Strange how many things that applied to. It was one of the ways in which she and Shannon were so different. Shannon was a devotee of speed—fast driving, fast skiing, fast living. Anything worth having was worth having *right now*. While Annie plodded straight from high school through college, Shannon raced off to Europe to find whatever adventures awaited her there. When she returned she threw herself into college, taking the maximum load, and then hurried on to law school. She got married along the way to a man she thought would love her forever, even though she'd only known him a few months. When that ended, she threw herself into being a lawyer. She was now a junior partner, having risen rapidly through the ranks of her firm. The pace of Shannon's life left Annie breathless. As much as she worried about Shannon's choices, she also tended to admire them. Unlike Annie, Shannon was unafraid of change.

"I don't like to go fast," Annie had told Mark, urging him to be patient. She wanted to wait until the time felt right to make love. Was that so unusual anymore? Apparently Mark thought so. No wonder he kept telling her he could wait all those months—he was getting it someplace else.

Shannon accused her once of going for the record as the oldest virgin who wasn't a nun or a science experiment. Annie saw no reason to rush. When she finally did give her virginity to a man she'd been friends with for several years, she called her cousin sobbing. "It was terrible! Why did I do it?"

"Was he that bad?"

"No! I don't know—maybe. I just wish I hadn't used it up."

"What?"

"My first time. I won't ever have that again."

"Most people are thankful about that."

"I should have waited."

"I should come down there and slap you."

Even now Annie could count her lovers on two fingers. She'd tried dating a few men, but none of the relationships took hold. She slept with one of them a few times, but there was no magic in his touch. After a month of trying, they both decided to move on. After that, Annie adopted a strict policy of keeping her clothes on until she knew where the relationship was going. So far that had resulted in never dating a man for more than a month.

Which was why Mark had seemed so promising. Four months of steady dates, of comfortable companionship, of slowly-developing desire. Annie had planned on surprising Mark with a night of tender lovemaking on their six-month anniversary, but they never made it that far.

Just as well, Annie thought. He obviously wasn't right for me.

She could feel herself beginning to relax. Being tethered to Kjartan worked better than Annie hoped—funny how a little leather strap could make her feel so secure. With the steering and speed taken care of, she could focus on details, like keeping her shoulders loose and her spine straight. She could have ridden with her eyes closed, Annie thought. Kjartan would look after her.

The horses jostled against each other as they trotted, pinning Annie's leg between them and pushing it hard against Kjartan's. She felt as though her knee were being crushed between two trucks.

"Does it hurt?" Kjartan asked after her third grunt.

"No," Annie lied, "it's fine." She wondered if she would wake up the next morning with a dent in her calf the shape of Kjartan's knee.

But then they came up over a rise, and suddenly the land-scape distracted her from the pain. For the first time in her life she was utterly, outrageously awed.

To her right, no more than two steps away, the earth dropped toward the ocean a thousand feet below. The white foam of arctic waves bubbled over a black sand beach. If she had been riding on her own, untethered, she might have swooned at the sight of so much cliff so near. But trusting Kjartan's horse to keep her own from pitching over the edge, Annie unwedged her leg from Kjartan's and leaned over to see more of the view.

"This is spectacular."

"I wish it was clear," Kjartan grumbled, gesturing toward the clouds. "You could see so much more."

"I don't need more."

"When it's clear, you can see the peaks over there. Petra!"

Kjartan called something in Icelandic. Petra answered in the same. After a few more sharp words from Kjartan, Petra nodded somberly and waited for him to take over the lead.

"She always tries to take the short cut here," Kjartan said. "I tell her people want to see more. She's always in a hurry." He urged his horse forward. Kjartan and Annie moved into the lead. "This way," Kjartan scolded his assistant.

Annie saw that the trail Petra chose would have taken them down into a swale, away from the cliffs. Kjartan's route kept them close to the edge, the better to see the black sandy beach below.

"A long way down," Annie observed.

"That's where we're going," Kjartan answered.

To go from here to there seemed a project longer than one night, but Annie didn't question it. In fact, she didn't feel the need to question anything. Riding along linked to Kjartan, she felt secure, protected. If he had told her the horses would leap now, out into the void, but that they would land quite safely on the beach below, Annie thought she might have believed him.

Soon the narrow cliff trail led them to a wide, flat expanse of tall grass and equally high yellow flowers. The horses dipped their heads to tear off the top morsels.

"First stop," Kjartan said.

The riders dismounted. Kjartan instructed them to pull the reins over their horses' heads, but to hold on to them while the horses grazed in case any of them decided to bolt. Kjartan unclipped the tether between the two bridles, and Annie followed her horse as it sampled the great grasses of the highlands.

Sophie coaxed her horse toward Annie's. "How is your ride?"

"Fine—it's good. Thank you so much for telling me to say something. I don't think I would have liked it if I had to do those cliffs by myself."

"I thought Kjartan might give you a different horse. I didn't expect him to ride with you."

"Why not?"

"He never does. He tells Petra to take the beginners."

"He may still do that," Annie said. "I don't think he likes riding with me very much. He hardly says anything."

"He doesn't speak to anyone very much."

"He speaks to you."

Sophie winked. "It's because I talk to him first."

Annie decided to try it. When they were on the horses again, her leg pinned once more against Kjartan's, she cleared her throat and began. "How often can I ride while I'm here?"

"As much as you want."

"Can I go out every day if I want?"

"*Já.*"

"No?" The second she said it she caught herself. Her brain was just a beat slow in deciphering the sound. "Sorry—you said yes. It just sounded like...never mind."

"Yes," he repeated. Annie listened for any sign of annoyance, but didn't find it this time. "You can go out every day."

"Do you? Go out every day?"

"Yes, sometimes three or four times."

"Is it always big groups like this?"

"*Nei.* Sometimes just one or two people."

"You'd go out with just one person?"

"*Já.* If someone wants to ride, Petra or I will take him."

It sounded inefficient, but Annie didn't say so. What did she know about the economics of horse farming?

"I'd like to learn to ride better while I'm here. I'd especially like to learn the *tölt.*"

"I'll teach you tonight."

"Like this? On the tether?"

"Sure. But wait until later. It will be easiest to show you on the beach."

"What is *tölting*, exactly? I read about it, but I can't really picture it." The guidebook described it as a fast, smooth trot—a sort of fifth gear that other horses didn't have.

"My horse is doing it right now," Kjartan told her. "Can you see it?"

Annie studied the horse's legs. "Not really. It looks different, but I can't say why."

"You'll know it when you feel it. I'll show you later."

Now that the conversation was moving, Annie had lots of questions: about the breeding of the horses, the work on the farm, how severe the weather grew in winter. Between barking at Petra and shouting instructions to the other riders, he answered her without any sign of impatience.

"How long have you had your farm?"

"Eight years."

"Have you always been a farmer?"

"*Nei.* An architect. In Reykjavik."

The answer surprised her. "Really? How'd you end up here?"

"My wife's parents owned this farm. We used to visit, and I always liked it. I didn't like Reykjavik so much. Too big. When Marta's parents wanted to sell it and retire in Reykjavik, Marta and I decided to buy it."

"And now you run it by yourself?"

"*Nei.* I hire workers, like Rolph, who drove the van back to the farm tonight. And Petra. And a few more to help when I need it."

"Do you take people on rides all year long?"

"*Nei.* Just in the summer. Not so many people want to ride in the winter. The rest of the year I breed and train the horses."

"Do you breed them for sale?"

"*Já.* I sell a lot to Germany. Some to Norway and Sweden. Last year I sold ten to a woman who has a ranch in California. She wants me to come there in October to check on them and see if they need more training. I don't know if I'll go."

"Why? I would think leaving the cold here and going to California would be a great escape. Have you ever been there before?"

"*Nei*. I've never been to the U.S."

"California is close to where I live. It's nice there—lots of beaches, nice cool weather in the summers. October might be a little cold already, but probably nothing like it'll be here by then."

"I don't know if I'll go," he repeated. "My ex-wife lives there now."

"Oh. Sorry."

Kjartan shrugged. "Not your fault."

"Do you ever see her?"

"*Nei.*"

"Do you care?" The instant she asked it, she regretted it. "I'm sorry—don't answer that. I don't know why I'm asking you such personal questions."

"If it will make you feel better, I'll ask you some questions."

Annie squinted suspiciously. "All right."

"Are you married?"

"No."

"Ever been?"

"No."

"Boyfriend?"

"No."

"Why not?"

Annie sputtered. "What? I..."

"Okay," Kjartan interrupted. Annie caught his half smile. "The answer to your question is no, I don't miss her. I'm glad we were married long enough for us to buy the farm, but I'm not sorry we're not married anymore. I think she was right to leave. If she couldn't be happy, she should go."

"That's very generous of you."

Kjartan shrugged again. "No one wants to live with someone who is miserable." He quickly changed the subject. "The beach is just up there. Are you ready to try the *tölt?*"

They crested the slope. Ahead, stretching into the horizon, was the lava-black beach Annie had seen from the cliffs.

Sophie and Guy were already racing down its length, their horses in full gallop. Annie sincerely hoped that was not the *tölt.*

While the other riders let their horses open up on the long track of beach, Kjartan brought his and Annie's horse into a much milder pace. Annie's bones rattled as her horse trotted at this increased speed.

"Lean back," Kjartan instructed. "Pull his head up. Now squeeze your heels..."

For a moment the teeth-jarring trot disappeared, and Annie felt it: a smooth glide, a strange rhythm to her horse's hooves, the easy sway of the horse's hips.

And then it was gone. Right back to the miserable trot.

"Ugh," Annie grunted. "I lost it."

He coaxed her through it a few more times, but she never gained anything beyond the trot. "I have to stop," she said. "This is killing me."

Kjartan slowed the horses. Annie's teeth settled back in her head.

"This horse isn't so good at *tölting*," Kjartan confessed. "I didn't know you wanted to do that tonight. I'll make someone switch with you for the next beach."

"I don't want to take away anyone's horse."

"You won't—I will."

They walked the rest of the beach to save Annie's back from the assault of the trot. They joined the other riders, who were already on foot and allowing their horses to graze.

"Lunch," Kjartan said.

From the leather pouch on the back of his saddle he unpacked sandwiches, small boxes of orange juice, and a bag of fried bread strips that tasted almost like plain donuts.

Sophie's face was still flushed from the gallop. "Better?" she asked, nodding toward Kjartan. He stood talking to the Swedish parents.

Annie smiled sheepishly. "Yes. He's not so bad."

"Good. We're coming to the lava field next. I think it will be hard to ride side by side anymore. Maybe you can try riding alone now?"

"Do you think I'm ready?"

"Oh, yes," Sophie said. "This part of the ride is very slow

because of the rocks. You should try it—you might enjoy it much more."

Annie was surprised at her reluctance to give up the tether—not because she was afraid, but because she enjoyed Kjartan's company. Still, she needed to improve her skills on horseback, and riding alone seemed the next reasonable step.

Annie approached Kjartan before they mounted. "I think I'll try it alone for a while."

"Okay. Good. You should ride in the back."

"Will my horse let me?"

"*Já.* He was excited in the beginning, but now he will not be a problem."

Kjartan rode in front of her. He removed his hat and ran his fingers through his damp yellow-brown hair. Sitting astride his blond, California-tan horse, they both looked as though they had been painted with the same brush.

Watching the line of horses in front of her negotiate the uneven, sometimes steep terrain, Annie gained a new appreciation for the hardy, sure-footed breed. The few times her horse caught a rock the wrong way, he picked up his stride with barely the loss of a beat. Annie relaxed into the ride. She let the horse do its work while she scanned the wondrous landscape.

A photograph hung in Annie's house—the house she moved back into when her mother's health suddenly declined. It was a black and white photo of Annie and her three brothers, taken the year before her youngest brother Brian died. Annie was fourteen, Brian seven, her older brothers in their late teens.

For Christmas one year Annie had the photo reproduced and hired an artist to colorize it. He left most of the background black and white, and painted everyone's shirts wild, vibrant colors. She especially liked the bill on Brian's baseball cap, painted cherry red.

She thought of that now, looking across the lava field, its carpet of black rock such a sharp contrast to the bright green moss growing over it. Someone must have painted that shade of green—how else could it be so bright? The sky was silver-gray, adding to the black-and-white feel of the landscape.

She was tempted to call Kjartan back, to ask him to ride close to her again so she could ground herself in reality once more. She felt as though she were watching a movie through an old-fashioned projector that couldn't get any of the colors right.

Her horse stumbled, then quickly regained its footing on the rocky path. Annie snapped back to the work at hand. She was riding alone. She needed to pay attention.

Midway through the lava field, Kjartan called for another break.

"You all right?" he asked her.

"Perfect. No problem. This is a good horse."

Kjartan invited the tourists to follow him down the nearby slope on foot, while Petra minded the horses.

The slope was steep—as steep as some of the ones the horses had traveled, and Annie appreciated their skill all the more as she found herself stumbling over the rocks. She slowed down to keep from falling. The rest of the party kept pace with Kjartan.

She followed their voices to a gully, and found them standing at the mouth of a cave. Kjartan continued his story, about a fugitive murderer who had hidden there for many months before someone finally found him.

He led them deeper into the cave, until they stood in utter darkness. The German man flashed his lighter. Annie barely had time to adjust to the light before he doused the flame.

In that brief instant she saw Kjartan looking at her. She thought she might have seen him smile, but then the light went out.

Kjartan led them back outside. Annie walked slowly, dreamily taking in the unreality of the place. Just a few days before she had been sweltering in Tucson, trying to imagine what Iceland might be like.

Nothing like this, she mused. No amount of imagination could have conjured all of this.

She looked at her watch. Nearly 11:30 PM. The sky was gray, but still light. Clouds, rather than nightfall, accounted for the dusky cast.

An hour or so more to go. Annie's back ached mightily. Her thighs weren't so bad, but her shoulders and low spine screamed for rest.

Even though she was physically tired, Annie noticed she wasn't sleepy—strange for a woman who was usually in bed by 9:00. It's the light, Annie thought—it really does control you. Without darkness, the body missed its cue for sleep.

Once they were free of the lava field, Kjartan called for one last break. Annie watched him talking to the Swedish girl and her parents. From the look on the girl's face, Annie knew she wasn't happy with Kjartan's request.

He walked toward her, leading the girl's horse. "Try this one." He helped Annie into the saddle, then adjusted the stirrups for her height. "Do you want to try it alone?" he asked.

"No. With you." Annie felt silly for needing the crutch, but she also looked forward to riding with him again.

Kjartan told the others to go ahead. Then he urged his horse down the bank toward a beach so golden, Rumpelstiltskin himself might have spun it.

She felt it from the start: the smooth, rhythmic gait, the easy glide across the sand, the gentle sway of her hips.

She grinned at Kjartan. "Ahhh..."

"Faster?"

Annie surprised herself by answering, "Yes."

She had forgotten the pain of having her leg pinned against Kjartan's, but she was in no hurry for it to end. They pounded across the golden sand under a midnight sky still bright enough to read by. If she ever had the chance to feel like Freydis, this was it: her cheeks wet from sea spray, her skin chilled by the arctic wind, a tall blond Viking riding beside her. Pain was nothing— the ache in her back, the crushing of her leg—nothing would keep her from riding through the night. She had work to do— lands to conquer...

Annie, settle down.

She reined in her imagination before it could take her any further. Back to the pleasure of the moment—back to feeling the wind and the cold and the horse thundering across the sand and Kjartan's warm presence beside her.

Glad you came? she asked herself.

Wouldn't have missed it.

6

"Oo," Sophie said, her lips puckering like petals, "you don't look very good."

"Thanks." Annie hobbled to the cafeteria table and sat down.

Etta grinned. In a voice too loud for the morning, she asked, "Good, was it?"

Annie smiled, despite her pain. "Very good. Amazing. Beyond belief."

Sophie was kind enough to bring her a cup of coffee with copious milk.

"She was very brave," Sophie told Etta, although Annie wondered if a different story had circulated before she arrived.

The cafeteria was empty save for the three of them. "Where are the men?"

Etta answered, "You know where Wilhelm is—fishing, of course. Guy is with him today."

"Etta has offered to take me into town in her car," Sophie said. "Would you like to come?"

"Definitely. I need more aspirin."

"But you will ride again today," Sophie said. It was a declaration, not a question.

Annie shook her head. "I can't. I'm dead."

"No, that is why you must get right back on. You will feel so much better today. Now you know what you are doing. You will love it today."

"Sophie, I barely made it to bed last night. I was tempted to sleep in the grass."

Etta swallowed a mouthful of toast. "Listen to her. You should go out again."

"Why are you both torturing me?"

Sophie looked hurt. "You don't have to go if you don't want. But you did well last night. You will really like it today—I know you will."

Annie sighed. The truth was, if not for the ache in her back and legs, she really would like to go riding again. Now that she had felt the *tölt*, she was anxious to find it again. But at least a day's rest—wasn't she entitled?

Sophie laid the final snare. "You are here for such a short time..."

Annie groaned. "All right. You're right. Let me eat something and take some more aspirin. What time are we going?"

Sophie smiled triumphantly. "After lunch. Kjartan said he's taking a group at two o'clock. We'll have time to go to the town and then come back here and sit in the hot pool. You'll like that—it will ease your muscles."

The plan sounded attractive. Why not? Annie thought. Throw myself into the hands of these two and see what the day brings. It might be fun.

They assembled at Etta's car. "How far is it?" Annie asked.

"Thirty minutes only," Etta said.

The answer tickled some part of Annie's brain, but she couldn't make sense of the memory. She climbed into the back seat of Etta's brown sedan. Sophie turned from the front passenger seat and said warmly, "I'm so glad you'll ride again today. I promise you'll be happy."

Annie was happy. Until that moment she hadn't said it to herself, but it had been true for days. Ever since she awoke from her late afternoon nap on the day she arrived, she had felt a lightness of heart she couldn't put into words.

But now she wanted to try. "Is there a place to use the Internet here?"

"Kjartan has it in his house," Etta answered.

"No, I mean at a café, or maybe a library."

"No," Etta said, "I don't think so."

"We can ask at the store," Sophie offered.

Annie settled back and began composing the e-mail she would send to Shannon. Maybe by writing it down she would begin to understand what was happening to her. At the very least, Shannon would get a taste of this exotic place, and a feeling for the charm of the people Annie had met.

As the miles passed, Annie felt a strange sensation of having seen the countryside before. When they pulled into the store's parking lot, she knew why: It was the same parking lot where Kjartan had retrieved her—when? She had to think hard to remember. Had she been there only two days—three, counting today? It didn't seem right. Maybe the nearly-endless daylight was already playing tricks with her head.

Annie stepped from the car and scanned the area. "Is this the town?"

"Yes," Sophie answered. "They call it that. Not too big, is it?"

The town consisted of a store, a gas pump in front of it, a mechanic's garage across the road, a few houses, and a short row of office buildings.

Annie followed Sophie and Etta into the store.

"*Góðan dag,*" the female clerk greeted them.

"Hello," Etta answered.

"Hello," the clerk echoed.

Etta whispered to Annie, "I always let them know right away that I only speak English. It gives them time to fix their tongues."

The store was divided into three sections: a small dining area, a general store, and a video counter. A few patrons sat eating at the tables. A teenager stood eyeing the video selection. Etta and Sophie headed for the grocery shelves.

Annie wandered toward the video section, curious to see what American movies they might have. Other than a few titles with distinctively Icelandic lettering, Annie found the selection no different from the one at her neighborhood video store. A few covers indicated the movie had Icelandic subtitles, but most seemed to be standard-issue blockbusters, straight from Hollywood to this little outpost in the middle of the Icelandic countryside.

Annie joined Etta at the dairy case.

"You liked that *skyr* yesterday, didn't you?"

Annie agreed she had.

"Look at the flavors. Blueberry is best. You should try it."

The suggestion gave Annie an idea. "What food could that I try that's uniquely Icelandic—besides *skyr*?"

While Etta considered the question, Sophie offered her own list: *hardfiskur*, a kind of fish jerky; Icelandic chocolate with raisins and nuts; a hard liquor called *berserkja*.

"Ach, not the *berserkja*," Etta roared, much to Sophie's amusement. "That will tear out her eyeballs."

"It is very bad," Sophie admitted, "but you should try it so you will know."

"No, thanks," said Annie. "I can barely drink wine without passing out."

Etta grimaced. "It is the worst I have ever had. Do you know why they created it? To wash away the taste of rotten shark meat."

"That's true," interjected the clerk. "Have you tried it yet?"

Annie squinted at her. "Rotten shark meat? No. Are you serious?"

"It's very special," the woman assured her.

Annie handed her a package of *hardfiskur* and a chocolate bar. "I think I'll start with these."

Her transaction complete, Annie stepped aside for Sophie and Etta.

Sophie unloaded an armful of provisions: two apples, four bottles of carbonated, lime-flavored water, a package of chocolate-covered coconut cookies, and a string of condoms.

Annie averted her eyes from the last item, then privately ridiculed her own behavior. Why should she be embarrassed? What was wrong with Sophie buying condoms? Of course the two of them were having sex—Annie had never doubted it. But somehow seeing the evidence made her feel shy around the young woman.

Annie shook off the ludicrous discomfort. Sophie thanked the clerk and pocketed the condoms. The rest of the groceries she cradled in her arms. "You have to pay for bags," she explained.

Etta bought a package of gum and two containers of blueberry *skyr*. "One is for you," she told Annie. "Wilhelm can lick his fish."

The shoppers returned to the parking lot. Sophie and Annie waited while Etta pulled up to the gas pump and filled her tank.

"It's beautiful today," Annie said. The sun peeked through high clouds. The temperature was the warmest she'd felt since her arrival—maybe 50 degrees, 55.

"It was like this last week," Sophie said. "I'm sorry you've had only rain."

"This is like a winter day in Arizona. I love it."

Sophie nodded. "I want to go there some time. I would like to see the Grand Canyon. Do you live near there?"

"No, but if you come to Arizona you should come stay with me. I'll drive you there myself."

"That's sweet," Sophie said. "Would you ever come to France?"

Before last week, Annie would have answered "no" without thinking. The idea of flying over the Atlantic had never appealed to her, no matter how alluring Europe might seem.

"I don't know," Annie said. "Maybe."

Etta called to them in her hoarse, magnified voice.

Sophie checked her watch. "We still have time to visit the pool. How are you feeling?"

"Better. Not so stiff."

"Good. A hot swim will make you perfect."

Seeing Kjartan upon their return reminded Annie of her quest. "I forgot to ask about Internet at the store."

"I looked," said Sophie. "I didn't see anything."

"I'll ask Kjartan," said Etta, and she did so before Annie could object.

"*Já*. Yes. It's in there. Let me show you." He started toward the house.

Annie looked back at Etta, who made no attempt to hide her smile of satisfaction.

"Should I wait for you to go to the pool?" Sophie asked.

"Yes. I'll just have Kjartan show me what to do. Can I meet you in 15 minutes?"

Sophie agreed.

"You look tired," Annie told Kjartan. She unlaced her boots and slipped them into the corner.

"*Nei*. Not so tired."

"How much sleep did you get last night?"

Kjartan looked ceiling-ward to calculate. "Five hours. That's pretty good."

"Is that normal?"

"For summer." He led her down the hall toward the kitchen, and into the office. "Some nights it's only two or three hours. It's okay." He softened his eyes and smiled at her. "I sleep in the winter."

That look arrested her. It was the same direct gaze she had caught in the glow of the lighter inside the cave. As the moment lengthened, he still held his eyes on hers. Annie looked away, nervous.

Kjartan cleared his throat. "Click it here." He moved the mouse and pushed the button. Annie cleared her head for the lesson.

When she met Sophie again, her face was still flushed.

Sophie laced her arm through Annie's and started for the road. She inclined her head toward Annie's and said softly, "He likes you."

Annie stiffened, then tried to pretend she hadn't. "Who, Kjartan?"

"Do you know how I can see?"

Annie's heart pumped a little harder. "No."

"I have been here almost two weeks. I have been riding with him twice a day, and eaten meals with him, and seen him talk to people. He doesn't look at anyone. He just..." Sophie paused, seeming to search for the right words. "He is a zombie—do you know that word?"

"Yes, but I don't think he's a zombie. He might be shy—"

"No, it's something else. He has a—" Sophie pressed a fist to her heart and made a noise that sounded like *glunk*. "A hole here. *C'est mal*. He is unhappy. Do you see that?"

Annie no longer knew what she saw. What she *did* know was that she didn't want to lead herself on. Her mind was impressionable—her heart even more so. The suggestion that Kjartan might like her affected Annie more than she wanted it to. Hadn't she deluded herself enough with Mark? Why start the whole fantasy with someone new?

"I'm sure he's just being friendly," Annie said. "I'm a paying guest."

Sophie shrugged. "I don't think so. I think I know."

They entered the door to the *sundlaug* and paid the teenager sitting behind the counter. The women's dressing room was empty.

"You shower first before going in the pool," Sophie explained. She began undressing.

Annie turned her back and removed her clothes. She wore her bathing suit underneath.

Sophie walked naked into the showers. Annie followed, averting her eyes out of modesty—hers more than Sophie's.

"You should take your swim suit off," Sophie said. When Annie hesitated, she added, "It's your choice, but some people might look at you strange."

I'd look at me strangely, Annie thought, if I saw myself standing naked in a public shower with people around. If no other of her mother's lessons got through her brain, the one about public nudity certainly had.

Sophie pumped soap from the wall dispenser and lathered her hair and skin. Annie washed just her body, since she didn't intend to dunk her head. She realized this shower must be how the two campers freshened up every day.

Sophie wrung out her long brown hair and pulled a bikini over her wet skin. "Ready?"

The pool had a green cast to it. Annie noticed small chunks of what looked like algae floating on the surface of the pool.

"Uck. Is it dirty?"

"No, those are the minerals," Sophie said. "This pool is very healthy for you. Kjartan says it's one of the best in Iceland."

Kjartan again. Annie felt her face flush anew.

She lowered herself into the pool. The water was lukewarm—not at all as hot as she expected.

She spied another, smaller pool the size of a hot tub. Sophie was already out of the larger pool and heading for it.

"I like to switch," she said. "This one is too hot to stay in for long, but it will feel good on your legs. Come try it."

Annie joined her in the smaller pool and sank into the dark green water. Ahhhh. The heat seeped through her skin, deep into her bones. She rested her arms on the concrete ledge and closed her eyes. "Wonderful."

"Do you like Kjartan?"

Annie's eyes popped open. Sophie wore an angelic smile—so different from Etta's, but with the same devious intent behind it.

Annie narrowed her eyes. "Why?"

"Because I think you look like a good couple."

Annie huffed out a laugh. "He's not my type."

"What's wrong with him?"

Annie closed her eyes again, leaned back and pretended to relax. "I don't like blond men."

"That is all? You have no other complaint? Then I think you should look at him again."

"Why?" Annie felt her annoyance rising. She didn't need this charming, romantic-minded woman filling her head with useless ideas. "I'm on vacation. I'm leaving in a few weeks. I can't get involved with somebody."

"But what if he is right for you?"

Annie laughed, incredulous. "He's not! I don't even know him. He doesn't know me."

Sophie leaned back and stretched her toes to the opposite wall. "What if," she posed, "you and Kjartan were born to be in love? What if that is why you were compelled to come to Iceland?"

"It had nothing to do with Kjartan. I'm not looking for anyone."

"But what if it was your fate to find him now? Maybe all your life has led you to this place so you could be in love with the right man."

"Sophie." Annie softened her tone. "Sophie, you have to stop this." A slight pain flickered in Annie's heart. "It's not good for me. I can't think like this—it will only hurt my feelings."

"I think you should look at him again."

"I think we should go back now," Annie answered. "We'll miss the ride."

They walked toward the farm in silence. When they had almost reached it, Sophie asked, "Are you angry with me?"

"No." Annie stopped and faced her friend. "I don't want to be hurt again—it's too soon. I don't want to believe things that aren't true."

Sophie started to protest, but Annie cut her off. "Even if you were right—even if, let's say, he and I were meant to be together..." Her voice trailed off. She had intended to say, "It still wouldn't work. I'm going home soon. Nothing like this would work."

But what if—just for argument's sake—what if Sophie were right? What if every step Annie had ever taken, everything that had ever happened to her, had led her to this place right now? And what if the reason no one had ever been right for her before was so that she would be single right now, ready for this man to love her?

"Sophie, *please*. Don't talk to me about this anymore. My little heart can't take it."

Kjartan emerged from the stable as they entered the yard. "Ready soon?"

Sophie looked guiltily at Annie. "Yes. I have to change my clothes."

Annie nodded, silent. She headed down the footpath without waiting for Sophie.

"And you?" Kjartan called after her.

She kept her back to both of them, afraid to reveal the heat rising on her cheeks. "Yes," Annie answered, "I'm coming."

She wouldn't give Sophie the satisfaction of asking where Kjartan was. When Annie returned to the stable he and the van were gone.

Petra led the group of four—Sophie, Annie, and a Scandinavian father and daughter who didn't appear to speak English.

Annie rode a squat bay mare with a bushy black mane. The horse felt odd between her legs—too wide. Annie hoped her thighs would remold to this new horse quickly so she could settle in and be comfortable.

She didn't consider asking Petra for a tether. She wanted to try it alone—to prove to herself that she had already grown bolder with just a single night's ride.

Strangely enough, her aches seemed to disappear as soon as she was moving. Her body seemed to know more what it was doing. Annie stretched long from her waist and tucked her hips forward to pamper her low back. Maybe, she thought, riding twice a day wasn't such a foolish idea. Maybe by the end of her trip she would be riding as much as Sophie.

It was to be a two-hour trip, just to the beach and back, which suited Annie fine. She wanted to see the sand in the sunlight, to see if it truly were golden. She also wanted to try *tölting* on her own across the same stretch where Kjartan had cracked the code for her.

Only the father and daughter spoke, and even that was at a murmur, so Annie's mind was able to drift in the quiet of the afternoon. Even at what Annie took to be its full strength, the sun felt softer here than in Arizona. A sea breeze filtered over the heath, cool and damp. Annie wore the same black velvet helmet she had taken off early that morning. It was still wet from the rain.

Anxious to be free of the bone-jarring trot, Annie leaned back and coaxed the mare into a *tölt*. There it was, just as smooth and rhythmic as she remembered. Now everything was perfect.

When they crowned the grasslands, Petra paused for the horses to graze.

Sophie turned her horse toward Annie's before dismounting. The two women stood shoulder to shoulder while their horses tugged at the tall grass.

"How do you feel?" Sophie asked.

"You were right," Annie admitted. "I feel good. I'm glad I came out again."

"I'm always right." Sophie laid a friendly hand on Annie's shoulder. "You're not angry with me?"

"No. But I am curious about something."

"What is that?"

"All this talk about love and fate—tell me how you met Guy?"

"Mm. That is a nice story. We met on the train from Munich. We both visited friends there. I missed my train and had to take the later one, and Guy was on it. He came into the dining car and sat at the table across the aisle. I heard him order and knew he was French. We started talking, and..." Sophie smiled wistfully. "So you see?"

"See what?"

"It was fate that I missed my train. It was fate that Guy left that day, instead of the day before as he had planned. It was fate I went to the dining car and sat at that table. All so we could meet and be in love."

Annie eyed her skeptically. "But if you had caught the earlier train, maybe you would have met someone just as nice, and you would be with him now."

"No, I have met other men before, but I didn't love them. You see, only Guy is the right man for me. I might have met him when I was thirty or fifty or eighty, but he would always be the right man for me. I'm happy I met him when I did so I did not have to wait any longer. It was fate that we should find each other that day."

Annie wasn't convinced, but she saw no reason to argue with Sophie's romantic view of the world. Instead she asked, "Will you marry him?"

"Yes, I think, some day. It's not so important to me. I know I will be with Guy all my life now. I don't need to marry him. But," she added with a smile, "I would say yes if he asked me. If he said it was important to him, I would."

Petra signaled that the break was over. The riders remounted.

Within minutes they were at the beach. The sands seemed brown, rather than golden, in the daylight. Still, Annie wasn't disappointed. There in the full light she felt alive—energized— and ready to test her nerve.

Sophie charged along the shore, her horse racing into a full gallop. Her hair blustered from beneath her helmet. Annie knew if she could see Sophie from the front, the young woman's face would have been radiant with a smile.

The father and daughter hung back in consultation with each other. Petra waited behind them, keeping her chicks in a row.

Annie forgot everyone. She could feel the mare's muscles quiver as they took off across the sand. Briefly Annie endured the trot, then ahhh—there it was.

An image flashed across her mind. A Victorian aristocrat, waxed mustache, tall black hat. He sat erect in a small, open horse cart, his elbows neatly poised, hands in perfect position. His horse stepped high as they raced around a track. Where had she seen it? In a movie? Something on PBS? Annie lengthened her spine and held her elbows aloft. She felt born to the elite, a horsewoman by breeding. All from a simple change in stride.

She could have ridden for hours. Ahead of her she saw Sophie turn and race back toward her.

Bringing her horse along side Annie's, Sophie shouted, breathless, "I'll ride to the end with you."

Annie nodded. Sophie matched her speed. Now they were two sisters in a Jane Austen novel. Two high-spirited girls out for their daily ride.

On a beach. In Iceland. Not quite what Jane had in mind, Annie thought.

Too soon the beach disappeared. Rocks defined the edge. Annie recognized the slope beyond that led to a stretch of grassland. That was where Kjartan had asked if she was ready to try.

The two women turned their horses and *tölted* back to the start. Annie watched Sophie's horse from the side, appreciating the odd appearance of its stride. Now she couldn't remember what a regular horse looked like as it ran. Did it straighten its legs? Did it strike the ground at a diagonal, or did both legs on one side move together?

Annie knew then she would never ride any horse but this kind. She couldn't bear feeling anything other than this.

Back at the farm, the horses free of their saddles and rolling on their backs in the dust, Annie felt a rush of satisfaction. Who was this woman taking off her black cap, laughing with the French rider, striding across the stable as though she had done it a hundred times before? She had the strange sensation of being filmed. She stood outside herself and marveled at what she was becoming.

If only Shannon could see her now.

Back at the house, Etta was in the kitchen sipping coffee. Annie greeted her, but didn't pause. She continued toward Kjartan's office and booted up the computer.

While she waited for the screen to settle, Annie leaned against the doorway.

"Good ride?" Etta asked.

"Wonderful."

"Will you go out again tonight?"

Annie laughed. "No, I think I'm done for the day."

"Good. Then we can eat together. Petra is making salmon tonight. She will overcook it, of course, but I think we can still eat it."

Annie excused herself and went right to work. So much to tell. Where to begin?

. . .

KJARTAN STARTLED BACK TO ATTENTION. Where was he? The last few kilometers were a blank. Focus. Almost home.

It was catching up with him. He could go days without a decent rest, but eventually he had to pay. Not tonight, though. A group coming from Stykkishólmur. Maybe he could close his eyes for half an hour some time after supper. Maybe not. The days went like this.

Kjartan straightened in the driver's seat and concentrated on the road. Still, his mind couldn't help drifting back to where it had been moments before. One thought plagued him:

Why had he told her so much?

He never talked to anyone about Marta—what was the point? She had the right to leave, just as he had the right to stay. What made him want to talk to Annie about her?

He was sorry not to have ridden with her that afternoon, but he had put off getting supplies as long as possible. With the group coming tonight, and rides scheduled for the next several days with no break in between, Kjartan had to steal the time where he could.

What he needed, he thought for the hundredth time that month, were more employees. The business had grown enough that he needed a full-time cook in the summer, an extra stable man, an extra guide.

This would be Petra's last summer with him. She didn't know that yet, but Kjartan had decided weeks ago. Letting her come that summer had been a mistake. Her e-mails to him had hinted at affections he did not return. She had tried the summer before to make something happen. Kjartan rebuffed her politely, but perhaps, he thought afterward, too politely. He didn't want to give her any hope that their relationship would progress beyond what it was. He valued her presence as a hard worker, but he was always satisfied to say goodbye to her at the end of the season— to go back to living in the house alone, without having to worry she might knock on his bedroom door again in the middle of the night.

What, exactly, was he looking for in a woman? Petra was attractive, a skilled horsewoman, someone who came willingly to Iceland year after year. If it were companionship he wanted, she would fit nicely. But he did not want simple companionship. The horses, the land—they provided him with that. What he wanted—what he needed—was a reason to talk. In the winter he sometimes went days without saying anything but *gódan dag* to the horses. When guests began arriving in late spring, he had to loosen his tongue again, learn to make small talk, remember what people said to each other.

If he should ever find someone again—someone who wanted to live there and build the farm with him, to start a family and watch them grow—everything he had meant to do with Marta...

And then there was the physical. Marta had provided plenty of that in the beginning, but as her love for him cooled, so did her passion. By the end Kjartan suspected she made love to him only when she was bored and couldn't think of anything else to do.

He needed the physical, he conceded now, but even that was secondary to the kind of easy friendship he had always wanted from a wife. Someone he could relax with, who understood that silence did not mean anger or indifference. Someone who could love him through both summer and winter, without retreating like the sun.

His tires crunched on gravel. Petra leaned her rake against the railing and met Kjartan as he stepped out of the van.

"The group cancelled for tonight," she said.

Kjartan had never heard more beautiful words. "Good," he answered, his shoulders slumping. He already felt sleep coming on.

Petra smiled, as though his look of gratitude were for her. Kjartan turned away before she could say more.

He aimed for his office to see what tomorrow's schedule held. Annie looked up from his computer. She abruptly minimized the text on the screen.

"Hello," she said too quickly.

"Hello." Whatever it was she had been typing, she obviously

did not want him to see. A devilish streak made Kjartan want to stand there even longer, just to watch her discomfort.

"Did you have a good ride?"

Annie rested her hands in her lap. "Yes. I didn't like the horse as well as the one last night, but she *tölted* for me, so I was happy."

Kjartan picked up a stack of bills and casually sifted through them. He let the silence intensify.

From the corner of his eye he saw Annie drum her fingers against her thigh. Kjartan smiled inwardly. Why was he enjoying this so much?

"Um, did you need the computer?" Annie asked.

"No. I have work to do outside."

Still he didn't leave.

Now Annie smiled ever so slightly. "Okay, then."

Kjartan looked up. "Pardon?"

Annie interlaced her fingers behind her head and leaned back in the chair. Obviously she was willing to wait him out.

Kjartan pretended to find what he pretended to have been looking for. He pulled an envelope from the stack.

"See you at supper," he said.

"All right."

Annie waited until she heard the front the door close before she maximized the text once more.

"...You're going to think this is crazy, but I kind of like him. I can't explain it, but it's true. Hope all is well there. Don't do anything stupid."

Annie punched the send key, smiling at that last line. It was standard for their letters to each other, something they had begun doing when they were teenagers and had at least the chance of finding something stupid to do.

She leaned back and sighed. Her eyes roved the photographs on the wall. Whoever had taken them had a good sense of composition. Waterfalls dropped from clouds. Horses stood braced against the wind, their bushy manes feathering over their faces.

No pictures of people, though. No parents, no friends—nothing personal. Maybe that's how offices looked in Iceland. Still, Annie could not help thinking Kjartan was the kind of man who kept his personal life particularly well-hidden.

And why shouldn't he? Annie thought. His personal life was his own. She knew more about him than she should, thanks to Etta's introductory briefing. Annie wondered how Kjartan would feel if he knew how much Etta had told her.

"Do you ever see her? Do you care?" Why had she asked him that? Why had he answered? His marriage was none of her business. She would be more respectful of his privacy in the future.

Supper offered a wide menu of languages. Etta and Wilhelm spoke to each other in German, Sophie and Guy in French, Kjartan and Petra alternated between English and Icelandic.

"Your Icelandic is good," Annie told her. "How long did it take you to learn?"

"Ah, it's not so good yet," Petra said. "I'm still learning—it's hard. Even after all these years I don't understand everything."

Amidst the roiling conversation, Annie was strangely at ease. The unfamiliar words provided white noise. Annie ate and listened as to a symphony of voices. Only when someone spoke English did she know to pay attention.

Etta and Sophie took the trouble to translate anything Annie might find of interest. The truth was, Annie realized, she would have been just as happy to sit there the whole evening not understanding a word. She enjoyed being part of the group, but didn't feel a need to socialize just then. She preferred watching them, imagining them as characters in a foreign movie, trying to imagine her own place in that diverse, colorful crowd.

Kjartan seemed ready to fall into his plate. Annie felt a tenderness for him—a wish to take him gently by the arm and say, "Let's get you off to bed, poor thing." That emotion must have registered on her face, because she found both Etta and Sophie giving her significant looks throughout the evening.

For Kjartan's sake, Annie was the first to break up the party. "I'm tired," she announced. "I'm going to bed." Despite their protests she headed for the door and put on her boots.

From the sounds in the kitchen, no one else had taken the hint. Still, having said it, Annie realized she was enormously tired. She stepped out in to the crisp, moist air and picked up the foot path.

Clouds marred the blue sky, but the light still shone as though it were afternoon instead of 8:30 at night. Annie knew she should be tired—had convinced herself that she was—but somehow walking in daylight like that proved that she was wrong. She felt a second wind—or maybe a third one, by then—coming on. She opened the door to cottage 4 and retrieved her rain coat. What better time to go for a walk?

At the bottom of the cottage steps, she turned back and opened the door again. She pulled her bathing suit off the radiator and rolled it in a towel. She zipped the bundle inside her coat.

Amazing what steady daylight could do to a person, Annie thought. This must be the opposite of winter depression—a sort of summer high, everyone strung out on the light. No wonder Kjartan never seemed to sleep. He probably saved it all up for winter.

The door to the pool building was open, but the place was empty. Annie unrolled the towel and started changing out of her clothes.

Maybe it was the light, maybe it was the pleasures of the day, but for whatever reason, Annie seized on an idea. It was time to break out. Just a small thing, but something she wouldn't normally try. Iceland seemed to bring that out of her.

Annie stepped naked into the public shower. Hot water burst instantly from the spigot—no need to warm it up. The door to the building was unlocked, as was the one to the women's dressing room, so anyone could have walked in any moment. How her mother would have hated that.

She wasn't entirely relaxed, but she thought she might get there in time. A lifetime of modesty was difficult to erase in one quick move. She persevered though, and soaped and rinsed her entire body before turning off the water.

She could be bolder still. Wrapping the towel around her, she scooped up her bathing suit and headed outside.

Steam rose from the pools. A light drizzle fell from the sky. Covering herself with her towel until the last possible moment, Annie slipped into the smaller, hotter pool, fully buck naked.

She could hear her mother's voice in her ear. "That's how you get diseases! What if someone sees you? You're not that kind of girl!"

It took several minutes before Annie was comfortable unfolding her arms from across her chest.

Here I am, she thought. These are my breasts. Anyone can see them. Oh my gosh...

Deep breathing helped. She felt ridiculous for caring so much about something so trivial. She was certain Sophie had never suffered such angst—nor, for that matter, had Etta. She'd open her wide mouth with her enormous blocky teeth and laugh at Annie for being so repressed.

Annie decided to let Etta's voice drown out her mother's. This was Annie's time now, and she didn't want to waste it acting the same way she always had.

The rain chilled her head while the pool warmed everything else. She tipped her face skyward and let the drops drizzle down her neck onto her chest. Then, in an act of unprecedented audacity, she stood up out of the water—briefly, as quick as a subliminal message flashed on the screen—and exposed her breasts to the air.

Back into the water, a huge grin on her lips.

Oh, my, she thought. What's happening to you?

When the water was too hot to bear any longer, Annie reached for her bathing suit and her rain-soaked towel, and covered herself as rapidly as she could. Back to reality, she thought. She had gotten away with it so far, but no need to tempt chance.

Another brief rinse in the shower, then a combination of air drying and wiping down with the wet towel. She pulled on her silk-weight long underwear and then her jeans. In one last act of defiance, she stuffed her bra in her jean pocket and pulled her shirt over bare breasts.

Away from the hot pools the air seemed chillier. Annie pulled her hood over her head and zipped the coat to her throat. Then she headed back toward the farmhouse.

Still not sleepy, she thought. Normally a hot soak would do it, but not this time. She toyed with the idea of going back to the kitchen to see if anyone were still there. But her original reason for going had been to spare Kjartan a long night. That motive still held.

Annie returned to the cottage and made a better job of drying herself off. She changed into sweatpants, a fresh T-shirt, and thick socks. Then she retrieved the guidebook, and settled onto the futon to further her education.

An hour later she was still not sleepy. Her body was weary, but her brain wouldn't concede that it was nighttime.

Annie checked her watch: 11:00 PM—6:00 PM in Minneapolis. Shannon would have read her e-mail by now, and probably responded. What would she say about all of this? Annie had tried to be as truthful as possible in her reporting, down to the pressure she was getting from the German and French cupids. "You know I don't normally like blond men," Annie had written. "There's something sneaky about them." She knew Shannon would appreciate that, since her ex-husband was a blond.

But in a weak moment she had admitted to some small interest in Kjartan. "You're going to think this is crazy, but I kind of like him." No doubt Shannon would have something to say about that.

Annie went to the bathroom and looked out through the window toward the house. The lights were still on. Hopefully Kjartan had been allowed to go to bed, but maybe Petra was still awake.

No longer as reckless as before, Annie took a moment to slip on her bra. The rain had stopped, so she only needed the fleece jacket. She stepped back into the deceptive light and headed for the house.

Since it was so late she considered knocking, but then she worried she might wake Kjartan. She opened the door quietly and removed her boots, then glided on thick socks toward the office.

Kjartan sat at the desk. His hair was wet from the shower. He wore a threadbare T-shirt and loose cotton pants that looked like hospital scrubs. The eyes that met hers were rimmed with the red of exhaustion.

"What are you still doing up?"

"Just a little more to do," he answered. "I thought since I had a free night..."

"You look like you're about to fall over."

"I'm okay."

Annie stood there for a moment, her errand forgotten.

When she didn't leave, Kjartan asked, "Did you need something?"

"Oh. No. I was just going to—never mind."

"Going to what?"

"Check my e-mail. But I can wait till tomorrow." She shifted onto one foot, ready to retreat.

"I have to use this one because I need the printer, but you can use the one upstairs."

"No, really, it's fine. I'll see you tomorrow."

Kjartan was already on his feet. "It's no trouble. Come with me."

She didn't realize that "upstairs" meant his bedroom.

She didn't know what she expected, but this wasn't it. The room was tidy, softly-lit, masculine but not too. Wool rugs covered large sections of the wooden floor. Mahogany bookcases occupied one wall of the room, a bed and desk another. There didn't appear to be a closet, just a wide, dark armoire and a row of shelves for folded clothes. More clothes hung from pegs beside the bathroom door.

Kjartan's bed was actually two twin beds made up separately and bound together by a headboard. Each bed was covered in a red plaid comforter.

Two floor lamps added to the natural light coming through wide windows. The whole room had a soft, soothing glow.

"This is really nice," Annie said.

"*Já, takk.* Thanks. Computer's there."

She sat at the small desk beside the bed. "I won't be too long."

"Take your time."

Kjartan descended the stairs like a sleepwalker. His joints ached with fatigue. Seeing Annie's face in his doorway had proven a pleasant surprise. In his sleep-deprived state, however, he could not think what to do about it.

Annie accessed her e-mail account. Three new messages

since the afternoon: two from Shannon, one from the principal of her school.

Seeing the principal's name gave Annie a strange feeling of dread. Better to open the happy messages first.

The longer of Shannon's messages bore the subject line: "I'm so proud of you!" and contained words of praise for every new challenge Annie had described. She read through it with mounting satisfaction. Only Shannon could know how much this trip meant to her.

The second message, subject "Re: Kjartan" contained just three words:

GO FOR IT.

STEAM ROSE FROM THE KETTLE. Kjartan pulled a tea bag from the cupboard and made himself a cup. On impulse, he made a second one. Nothing to do then but take it to her.

Annie sat staring at the screen, rolling her bottom lip between her fingers. She looked up, distracted, then turned her eyes back to the computer.

"I brought you tea." He set it on the desk. "Everything all right?"

"Not really."

Kjartan sat on the edge of his bed and sipped from his cup. "Do you want to tell me?"

"It's my contract for next year. At the private school where I teach." She turned to him. "The thing is, I don't think I want to sign it."

"Is it bad?"

"No, it's the usual contract, I'm just not sure..." Annie sighed and shook her head. She gazed out the window. Kjartan thought he saw a hint of moisture in her eyes.

They sat there in silence for a while, both sipping their tea. Eventually Annie turned back toward the computer and shut it down.

"Do you ever think," she asked then, "that you're ready to move on, but you don't know how to do it?"

"I suppose so," Kjartan answered. "I was like that in Reykjavik."

"What finally made you leave?"

"This place. Marta's parents were ready to sell, and so I had my chance."

"I need something like that." Annie smiled sadly. "Maybe I should start looking at farms so I can quit my job."

"Why do you want to quit?"

Annie groaned. She leaned forward and rested her head in her hands. "I don't know—I don't know anything right now." She lifted her head. "Thanks for the tea. I'm sorry I've kept you up." She stood to go.

"You don't have to leave," Kjartan said. His eyes met hers. His gaze had a different quality this time—both gentle and intense. His voice was low. "Stay as long as you like."

Annie sank back into the chair. She didn't look away.

The moment lengthened. Annie's skin prickled. Her body felt heavy, rooting her to the chair. When he tipped his head slightly, gesturing for her to come near, she slowly shook her head.

He came to her instead. Took her face gently in his hands. Bent and brushed his lips against hers. The lightest touch. Barely a kiss.

Annie kept her eyes closed. "Danger," she whispered.

Kjartan drew back slowly. He knelt on one knee in front of her. He waited.

Annie wanted to open her eyes, but couldn't right away. A tingling lethargy spread through her. Her breathing was shallow. Light perspiration beaded her upper lip. When finally she could look at him again, she found him gazing at her with a tenderness she would never have expected possible—not from him, not from anyone.

Annie reached out and tucked a tuft of his yellow brown hair behind his ear. She left her fingers there, laid her palm against his cheek.

Her hand shook as she drew it back.

"I can't," she whispered hoarsely.

Kjartan caught her hand and kissed the open palm. Electricity shot through her limbs.

"I have to go," Annie said.

Kjartan held on to her hand a moment more, then released it. "Okay."

Standing felt like an unreachable goal. Annie braced herself against the arms of the chair and pushed up. Kjartan stood and stepped back.

She wondered what reserve of willpower might be strong enough to carry her back to the cottage. Her heart pounded. She needed to sit down—lie down—but certainly not here. If she could just leave—make it to her door—everything would be all right.

"Annie."

It was the first time she had heard him say her name. He opened the "a," making the word round and wide and lovely.

She turned.

He reached for her fingers, held them lightly the way he held his reins.

"I can't either," he said. "You're only here a few weeks—"

She nodded, desperate not to hear the rest. "Yes, I know. Good night."

"Good night," he said softly. Annie fled from the room.

She struggled into her boots and reached for her coat. The night air was as cold as she needed it to be. Her flushed face welcomed the chill.

The sky was just beginning to dusk. What time was it? Midnight? Morning? How was a person supposed to live like this?—nothing normal, nothing to hold on to. At night the sky was supposed to be dark—that was a given. But not here. Throw out the rules here.

Her boots crunched across the gravel, then onto the soft mud of the foot path. Behind her she heard the door to the house close. She dug her hands into her pockets and walked faster.

"Annie." Again the soft round tone. She pretended not to hear.

He followed her to the steps of her cottage. Waited there. Annie climbed onto the porch. She stuck her key in the door.

Her hand was on the knob, so close to opening the door, ducking inside, shutting him out.

Annie leaned her forehead against the door. "I'm so...things are so strange for me here."

Kjartan mounted the steps slowly. Annie could barely breathe.

She turned, wanting him to be there.

He wrapped his arms around her and pulled her close, already kissing her. Annie gave in to softness of his lips, the warmth of his mouth, the pressure of his body against hers. She surrendered to the uncertainty of it all. She opened up to him as if they were already lovers, as if kissing him were something she had already done a hundred times before. As if to kiss him like this was the only reason she had come to Iceland.

They stood under the narrow eaves, Annie leaning against the door, Kjartan supporting her with an embrace both sturdy and soft. Annie let go. She let her body mold against his, let his hands move where they would, let herself want everything he might ask of her.

She reached behind her back and fumbled at the knob.

"It sticks," Kjartan whispered.

"I know."

Keeping his mouth on hers, he covered her hand with his and grasped the key. He pulled the door forward while turning the lock. Then they were inside.

He slipped her coat from her shoulders as they moved across the room. He sat on the futon and pulled her onto him. She straddled him, hungry for his mouth, her hands gripping his hair.

Kjartan slipped his hands beneath her T-shirt and underneath her bra. He lifted them clear in one movement, his soft lips already at her nipple.

Annie didn't speak. She didn't want to hear herself say anything. She was afraid she might tell him to wait, to stop, to think about it.

He lifted her arm and licked the curve of her armpit. She nearly screamed with the bizarre pleasure of it. Then he held both breasts, gently kneading one while teasing the other with his tongue.

She lifted his shirt away and ran her hands along his smooth chest. In the light from the window above them she could see the muscles of his stomach, the strength in his shoulders and arms. She bent forward and slipped his nipple into her mouth, wondering if he found the same pleasure in it she did.

Kjartan brought his mouth back to hers. His tongue was hot, his lips warm. Annie could hear her own breath, panting, quick. She guided Kjartan's mouth back to her breast.

She was watching him now, watching how he touched her, studying his face in the soft twilight. With each moan his eyes half closed. Each time he opened them again he gazed into hers. Annie looked back, unashamed.

The thin cotton of Kjartan's pants did nothing to hold him back. Still in her sweatpants, Annie pressed as close to him as she could, wanting to feel his excitement. She shifted her hips, causing another low moan, his brown eyes disappearing behind blond lashes.

Annie felt a need so great it threatened to overtake her. But even then, even when her body ached for him almost more than she could bear, Annie's head demanded she be rational.

Pulling her mouth away from his just enough for her lips to move, she said, "I can't...I didn't bring...I'm not on birth control." Right back to his lips. Why would she ever want to leave them? But she murmured one thing more. "Unless you have..."

"No...not for a long time...didn't think I would need it."

Knowing they wouldn't make love that night relieved Annie of any lingering inhibition. She threw herself into the moment, relishing the feel of his lips, his hands, his bare chest against her breasts.

She rocked her hips rhythmically, pushing their desire to the limits. Kjartan moaned and buried his lips in her neck. Annie pressed against him, felt the perfectly-matched contours of their bodies, imagined how it might feel to have him inside her. He sucked at her breast again, hungrily pulling her into him, his hands on her back, guiding her. Up, down, again.

Annie's eyes opened wide. She felt as close as she ever had to dropping over the edge into orgasm. Just a little more...would she finally feel it this time?

Kjartan panted, his body on the verge. Annie held his face in her hands and moved slowly, achingly slowly, until he could hold on no longer. He groaned and shot his pelvis forward, gripping both of her breasts as his body tensed, then finally released.

She could feel the sweat on his back, on her chest as she pressed it against him. She kissed him long and deeply, savoring what was left of his shuddering moan.

Kjartan held her at the ribs and continued kissing her, lightly now, sweetly, tenderly.

Annie allowed herself a smile. In another place, another world, she might have felt shy. But she was not herself at the moment, and for that she was truly grateful.

He intertwined his fingers in hers. She followed his gaze to her breasts. Then he lifted his eyes to her face again. His smile was softer than she had ever seen.

"I'll go to the store tomorrow," he said.

"Buy a lot."

"Already thought of that."

Kjartan folded her in his arms. Annie rested her cheek on his chest and listened to the echo of his heart.

In another world Annie would have asked questions now: What happens next? What does this mean? But here she didn't want to know. She gave in to the strangeness of it all. In a land where the sun still shone after midnight, why should she expect anything to be normal?

Slowly they came back to their senses. Still straddling him, Annie leaned backward and retrieved her shirt from the floor. He helped her pull it on, kissed her again as her head poked through.

At the door they kissed again, kissed more, neither of them anxious to break the spell. When she closed the door behind him, she leaned back against the sink in the tiny kitchen and waited for the fog to clear. She listened to his footsteps on the wooden stairs, imagined him walking across the wet grass, back onto the dirt path, across the gravel to his door.

When enough time had passed that she imagined him inside and upstairs in his room, she bent to untie her boots. Both had neglected that formality. She could see their muddy boot prints leading to the futon.

She lay on her bed in the dusky light, imagining everything

that had just happened happening again. Start at the door. Wait for him to come up the steps. Turn. Wait for him to kiss you. Open your arms.

It wasn't until later that she realized what a mistake she had made.

8

"*Guten morgen*," sang Etta, much too pleased with herself.

Annie didn't pause at the table, but went straight to the coffee urn and poured her first cup. She used the time to settle her expression: Since awakening Annie had been smiling *way* too much.

She turned and looked at them all as blankly as she could. "How did you all sleep?"

"*Trés bien*," answered Sophie. She rose and kissed Annie on the cheek, whispering, "And you?"

Annie drew back and scrutinized the crowd. They knew something—she was sure of it. The thought didn't please her. Like cradling a butterfly in her hands, Annie wanted to treat her emotions over the night delicately, afraid she might scare herself away.

Wilhelm wore his branded smile. "Today," he said, "you are mine. No excuses. You can't come to Iceland without fishing."

Etta barked, "She does *not* want to fish."

"I don't know what I'm doing yet," Annie said. "Let me wake up first."

Sophie caught her eye. Did that smile mean something? Annie leapt nervously from the table. "Let me get something to eat. Are you all done already?"

"No, no, take your time," Etta said. She lifted her cup and drank. "No hurry."

Of course you're not in a hurry, Annie thought. You've all been waiting to pounce on me.

She was grateful for an excuse to turn her back on them. She hadn't counted on anyone knowing what had happened. What had been Kjartan's and her secret alone, seemed to have spread in the few hours she slept.

Annie assembled what had become her favorite breakfast: toast with cheese and jam, *skyr* and fruit—raspberries in syrup this time—a glass of watery orange juice, a few sections of sliced orange.

Okay, she bolstered herself, take control of this. You don't have to tell them anything you don't want to. This is private. You're entitled to keep it to yourself, no matter what torture they have in store.

She adopted a bright smile and returned to the table. "So. What is everyone doing today?"

How was he going to tell her?

Kjartan rode at the front of the group, trusting his horse to keep to the path. He knew he should be friendlier—keep the customers happy—but their impression of him was the last thing on his mind.

They were all Americans, part of a bus tour. Two men, three women. All claiming some experience with horses, or he would have brought Petra, too.

The women were hideous. Loud, demanding, condescending. What was he, after all? A poor dumb farmer whose English was not what it should have been. The schools in Iceland began teaching English when children were eleven. Like other students, Kjartan also learned Danish and Norwegian. Language had never been his strong subject. He was a mathematician, a draftsman, a tinkerer. He would rather spend his time taking something apart, designing something, working with his hands, than expanding his English vocabulary.

These people talked to him as though he were an idiot—one who was hard of hearing as well. They moved their lips in exaggerated enunciation, speaking loudly as though that were the secret to being understood by a foreigner.

All he wanted to do was think of Annie, but these people kept demanding his attention.

Is my stirrup right? This helmet is wet. Why can't I wear my own riding boots? No one told me I had to disinfect them. The horses looked smaller in the pictures. I thought they were supposed to be ponies. Must be nice—you get to ride all day instead of having to work.

These were the kind of people who had charmed Marta away. She admired their ridiculous confidence. When the offer came to sell a few horses to a rancher from California, Marta's mind must have already been working. She would get out—finally. Leave the dark, depressing winters, leave her brooding, boring husband. She was gone within a month of the sale.

"Just to check on the horses," she had lied.

September, October, November—"Please, just a few more weeks." That pouty voice. "I'm having such a good time. Don't make me come home." When did he realize he had lost her? Before the papers came from the lawyer, but not much before. Kjartan had always been slow to understand women.

Oh, Annie. What are you thinking? What should we do?

He saw his choices like this: They could become lovers—that day, even, if he finished with this group in time to go to the store. Other riders were coming after lunch. Then the rescheduled night ride. Kjartan might squeeze out an hour to go to town between groups, but just barely.

And then what? How far could this thing go? She was leaving in two weeks. Even if theirs could be the greatest love affair Iceland had known, what chance did it have once she left? He supposed he could visit her, maybe for a week during the winter if he could find someone to look after the farm. A week was hardly time enough to nurture a love.

He could ignore the future. Give himself the gift of these two weeks without pretending there would be more. He had not made love to a woman in six years—*six years*—since Marta left. What man lived like that? He had not forgotten how it felt to touch a woman, to taste her, to move inside her, but at some point he had lost the will to make it happen. He couldn't imagine going through it again—the awkward courting, the gradual opening of his heart, the danger that everything would fall apart, leaving him lonelier than when he started.

Danger. Annie had said it herself, at a time when both their minds were still alert. She knew as well as he did that nothing could come of this—nothing but a few weeks of sweet pleasure, followed by the gloom of separation.

No. He would be wise this time. Keep his heart to himself, no matter how tempting the possibilities. No doubt Annie felt the same. She was an intelligent woman, and had probably experienced her own share of hurts. If anyone could understand the folly of continuing, she would.

"Do you have something to tell me?" Sophie asked when they were alone. They had lingered late at breakfast, promising to meet the others back at the house. A rowdy group of Czech teenagers filled the other tables. They would be spending the next few nights sleeping in sleeping bags on the floor of the gym. During the day they went sightseeing by bus.

"These children are allowed to smoke?" Annie asked. Two teenagers sat with one of their adult escorts, all of them puffing away.

Sophie turned to look. "Yes. Everyone in Europe smokes."

"Not you."

"No. I always hated it. Annie, you're ignoring me."

"I'm not. I don't have anything to say." She was sure her cheeks were as red as the coat hanging from the back of her chair.

Sophie refused to relent. "The walls of my tent are very thin. I heard Kjartan call to you. I looked, of course."

Annie's mouth went dry. "What did you see?"

Sophie leaned across the table and laid her hand over Annie's. "Don't worry. I didn't tell anyone."

"Etta seemed to know."

"Etta has ears like a satellite, she's only two cottages away from you, and she never sleeps. She said she heard your door close and looked out to see whether it was you. She saw Kjartan leave."

Annie rested her forehead against her hand. "Does everyone know?"

"No, only Etta and me—and Guy, of course."

"Of course. Maybe I should go fishing with Wilhelm today. He'll be the only one not looking at me funny."

Sophie smiled. "Now tell me, since I already know."

Annie shook her head. "I don't know. I just—something happened last night, but I'm not sure what it means."

"It means whatever you say. Do you like him?"

"Very, very much."

"So then."

Annie laughed. "So then what?"

"That is all you need to know. You like him, he likes you, today is another day. You will see what you do next."

"But there's no future in it," Annie protested. "This is foolish. We didn't—" She leaned forward and whispered. "—make love last night, if that's what you think. We just—" Annie smiled shyly. "Well, it wasn't that. And I'm not sure we should go any further. I don't have one-night stands—do you know what that means?"

"Then let it be more than one night."

Annie felt the color rise on her throat. "Maybe it shouldn't be any night at all. I'm not like this, Sophie. I don't sleep with men I've just met."

"I didn't think you did. But this is special. Why don't you see what will happen? Maybe you should take a risk."

"I don't know." Annie leaned back to signal that the interview —the interrogation—was over. "We should go."

They scooted their chairs out from the table and strolled past the smoking teens. Annie heard snatches of the Czechs' conversation— yet another language she would have been happy to sit and listen to.

When they arrived back at the house, they found Wilhelm, Etta, and Guy standing at the base of the manure pile in front of Kjartan's stables.

"What are you doing?" Annie asked.

Wilhelm grinned. "Searching for worms."

"Come dig in this pile of crap with us," Etta cajoled. "What else could you do that was better?" She wiped her hands against her pants. "I must love you too much," she told her husband. "I could be sitting in a spa instead."

"Will you come with me, Annie?" Wilhelm asked.

"Not today, but I will soon—I promise."

"Tomorrow we drive to Breidafjordur," he informed her. "I'm meeting a friend who will take me out in his boat. Etta doesn't like the boat. Would you like to come with us—see more of Iceland? You will make Etta happy."

Annie's first instinct was to decline. The truth was, she wanted to spend time with Kjartan—to be available if he had time for her.

She hated women like that. They were the ones who couldn't make plans until they knew whether their boyfriends were taking them out. Annie had played runner-up too many times to enjoy doing it now to someone else.

"Yes, I would like to go. That would be nice."

Etta beamed. "Wonderful! I won't have to sit in the car reading a book."

"I expect you to fish," Wilhelm warned. "I can't allow you to leave Iceland until you do."

"I'll fish," Annie promised. "As long as I don't have to sift through this crap."

She cast an eye toward the stable. Petra was inside cleaning the tack. The van was parked in the driveway, so Kjartan might be out in the pastures somewhere or out on a ride.

"When are you riding today?" she asked Sophie and Guy.

"I think Kjartan said he would go out at one o'clock," Sophie answered. She shouted the question to Petra. The redhead emerged from the stable holding the bridle she had been scrubbing.

Perhaps she was just oversensitive this morning, but Annie felt certain Petra had looked at her strangely. "We go at two o'clock," Petra said. "Kjartan or I will lead."

If Petra was leading the ride, Annie thought, that meant Kjartan might be free. They could talk, feel out the situation. If Kjartan was leading, Annie wanted to go with him, to spend time someplace beautiful with the man who was winning her heart.

"Can I tell you later?" Annie asked Sophie. "I'd like to relax for a while. Read. Catch up on my e-mail."

"Okay. I'll meet you later."

True to her word, Annie strode toward the house to use the computer. She wasn't sure what she would say to Shannon, but she felt a report was appropriate.

A stack of sealed envelopes crowded the edge of the desk. These must have been the bills she saw Kjartan paying last night. The poor man worked too hard. He needed more sleep. He needed more love.

One new message, from a girlfriend. The contract from Annie's principal still sat in her saved mail.

What was she going to do about that?

Of course she would sign it, wouldn't she? She had already committed to the new year. If she said no now, they'd have to scramble to find a replacement. That wouldn't be fair. Besides, what else would she do but teach there? The other schools would have already staffed their faculty for the fall.

Annie indulged in the "what if's." What if she told them she wouldn't renew? She could move someplace else for once in her life—maybe Minneapolis, maybe Denver to be closer to her brother James. There would be lots of schools to choose from there. She could spend the year getting recertified for a new district, and start fresh at a new school a year from now.

What if...

She was almost afraid to think it. But thinking was all right—no one would know. It wasn't like writing on the cover of her notebook, "Mrs. Kjartan Thor-whatever" or "Annie Thor..." Actually, she thought, she might have to become Annie Alansdottir. She hated the idea of her name sticking out in the phone book.

Aarg. Don't be stupid. You're not going to be Mrs. Kjartan anything. This is what it is: A passion. A fling. A deep and mysterious love that lasts only a few weeks.

Annie opened a new page and wrote to her cousin. She kept the details clean, and included a description of her first experience skinny-dipping. She was sure Shannon would be proud of that.

"*So here I am,*" she concluded, "*my little heart wanting him to love me, my body screaming for some more attention, my head utterly empty of any good ideas about how to make this work. I took your advice and went for it. Now here we are. Any more brilliant ideas?*

"*Don't do anything stupid. (I'll try not to, either—at least not until I hear from you.) xxoo A.*"

Annie checked the clock. Nearly 11:00 AM, so Shannon was probably just waking up. She enjoyed the idea of this e-mail greeting her when she booted up her computer. Every day should start with a little romance.

With that in mind, Annie scanned the stable yard and the pastures on the way back to her cottage. No Kjartan. Maybe if she were patient he would come find her.

Patience is overrated, she thought. I want to kiss him *now*.

Kjartan stormed into the house.

Why did he let them get to him?

"You...speak...very...good...English. Go-o-o-od," one of the American women had enunciated for him. He glared at her with disgust.

Her husband handed Kjartan a twenty dollar tip. "Anyplace we can get some decent food?"

Kjartan might have offered to have Petra cook something for them. He might have told them to try the small restaurant owned by a family he knew. He could have directed them to the store at the crossroads where they could find groceries as well as a café.

"*Nei,*" he answered, pocketing the money. "No good food around here."

"Didn't think so," the man chuffed. He slapped one of Kjartan's horses on the rump. "Good little ponies you've got here. A nice ride."

Kjartan bristled at the word "ponies." Icelanders were particularly sensitive about this false description of the ancient Viking breed. He didn't bother correcting the man, though. People like that weren't interested in learning.

Kjartan strode to the house without any further formality. If they needed something more they could ask Petra.

He took the stairs two at a time. If he were lucky he could have a few minutes of peace now. He wanted nothing more than to close his door, lie on his bed, and get away from them all for a while.

A folded sheet of paper decorated his pillow. Kjartan felt his stomach tighten, knowing whom it was from.

What was he going to do?

"I can't stop thinking about you," the note said. Kjartan refolded it, then folded it into a smaller square. He stowed it in his pocket along with the twenty dollar bill.

Then he lay back on the bed and stared at the ceiling.

No good to let it go on. He had to tell her soon.

ANNIE SNACKED on dried fish and smooth Icelandic chocolate. She was glad she had purchased both. Just as the alcohol she had seen in the store was used only to wash away the taste of rotten shark meat, so the chocolate must have been intended to balance out the taste of *hardfiskur*. The jerky wasn't anything like she expected. It tasted dusty and too fishy. Yet she ate half the bag. She would have to buy groceries to keep in the little refrigerator, or start packing a lunch from the breakfast supplies. Now that her body was finally used to the change in time zones, it wanted its three meals on schedule.

Close to 2:00 she brushed her teeth—twice, to remove the film of dusty fish—and changed into her riding jeans.

She could not stop smiling.

The whole thing was too incredible—to have come there on a whim and find such a warm, intelligent, stimulating man. Shannon was right: There was something to be said for impulsiveness.

One look told her everything.

She crested the slope of the footpath and caught his eye from a distance. He looked away, obviously not happy to see her.

In fact, so obviously, Annie stopped in her tracks.

No, I'm imagining things, she thought. She drew up her

courage and came closer. Kjartan barked out an order to Petra then stomped into the stable.

He's tired, Annie thought—no wonder. He's had a bad morning. It has nothing to do with me.

When he emerged from the stable she was there, waiting for him. Before her smile could fully form, Kjartan stalked right past her with barely a nod. He muttered something that might have been her name.

A shiver of realization swept through Annie's veins. He doesn't want me. It was a mistake. The whole thing was a mistake.

She turned and strode back to the footpath as calmly and naturally as she could. Sophie and Guy met her part way.

"Are you going?" Sophie asked.

"No. Maybe later. Not today." She resumed walking to avoid any further questions.

When she was safe in the cottage, Annie pulled off her boots and sank onto the futon.

What had happened? Just hours before they had been in that very spot, both of gripped by a passion Annie thought was real.

It was a trick of the light. Nothing here was real. Everything abided by some strange set of rules Annie didn't comprehend.

Stupid, she thought. Stupid. No wonder Shannon had left off their usual parting line of "Don't do anything stupid" when she sent her e-mail about Kjartan.

Go for it.

The stupidity was implied.

9

<hr>

Hunger drove her to the house.

She had two choices: She could hide out the rest of her vacation, rationing her *hardfiskur* and chocolate, or she could enjoy herself despite her grave error.

What would Freydis do? she asked herself. Freydis would take a sword to his heart and slice it into bits.

And she wouldn't dare miss a meal on some man's account.

Annie braced herself and headed for the house. It was 6:00. Sophie and Guy were still in their riding clothes.

"Ah, you missed a wonderful ride," Sophie mourned. She handed Annie a carrot stick and bit into her own. "The waterfalls were huge. We saw a mother sheep and her babies. They came up close enough we could have worn them for coats."

Annie was relieved not to find Kjartan there.

"What's for dinner?" she asked.

"Potatoes, fish, salad, bread—same every night." Sophie handed her another carrot stick. "Guy's horse ran off with him."

Guy grinned sheepishly. "Yeah, well, I lost concentration."

"He lost a stirrup," Sophie corrected, "that was the problem. And then the horse *shoom!*" Her hand rocketed through the air. She and Guy were both laughing now. "And I yelled, 'No, wait!' because I thought he was going the wrong way, and so I chased him." She bent over, one hand holding the imaginary reins, the other slapping her invisible horse's rump. "And he yelled, 'I can't stop it!'" Both pealed with laughter. Sophie held her hand to her belly. "And I rode faster, faster—" She applied the whip to the invisible horse's flanks. "—and then his horse—"

"Stopped," Guy said. "For no reason."

"Yes, for a reason," Sophie protested. "It was because I was there to save you and he knew he had no chance to get away."

Guy looped his arm around her waist and pulled her close. He kissed her fondly and said, "Thank you, my brave Sophie. You saved my life."

"I know I did," she agreed brightly. "Now you will have to do my wash tonight."

Annie's heart endured a dull ache. So sweet to see the two of them, but so very hard as well. Maybe love truly was for the young. By the time someone was Annie's age—or Kjartan's— maybe they'd seen too much to be this sweet and loving and...happy.

Kjartan breezed through the kitchen only long enough to retrieve the sandwiches Petra had left in the refrigerator. Annie counted eight. She wondered if Kjartan assumed she would be part of the group.

He swept past her without a word—without even a glance in her direction.

Sophie's look of confusion must have matched her own. Annie shrugged and smiled as though everything between she and Kjartan were understood. Inside, her heart hit the floor.

Sophie had the grace to say nothing about it. She pulled a loaf of bread from the oven and tipped it into a basket. Then she removed the platter of fish and set it on the counter. "Petra's going out with them tonight, so we have to serve ourselves."

Annie had just sat down to her meal when Kjartan reappeared. He asked her brusquely, "Are you coming tonight?"

Numb, Annie shook her head.

Kjartan turned and left without another word.

The blood drained from Annie's face. She couldn't imagine what she had done to invite such coldness.

"He is not himself today," Sophie consoled. "I could see it on our ride."

"No, I think he is himself," said Annie. "I think this is exactly who he is."

The next morning she was grateful for a reason to leave.

Kjartan had not come to her. She hadn't really expected him to, but some small hope lingered that once he returned from his ride he would climb the steps to her cottage, knock softly on the door, and in the same tender voice he had used the night before, explain everything to her.

But he did not come. So. That was that.

She shared an early breakfast with Etta and Wilhelm, then packed into the back of their car for a day's outing. A few miles down the road from the farm, Annie felt her anxiety ease. She had been afraid of seeing him that morning—of seeing that cold look of...what? Dismissal?—and not knowing what to say, how to act. But he was either still in the house or already off somewhere, and Annie was spared having to mimic indifference.

"It will rain today. Will you be warm in that?" Etta's jarring, crackly voice cut through Annie like a chain saw.

"Yes, I'll be fine." Annie wore long johns underneath her jeans. She had brought rain pants as an extra layer if needed.

Her gut ached. Not surprising, she thought, considering its proximity to her heart. But she wondered if there were more to it than that.

"Will we be going past the town?" Annie asked. "Past the store?"

"Yes," Wilhelm answered. "I'll stop there for coffee."

Annie tried to picture her calendar at home. Written on one of the boxes would have been the letter "P." In her mad rush to purchase tickets, find accommodations, arrange for someone to pick up her mail and paper and water her plants, pack for the weather without packing too much—in the midst of all the planning, she had forgotten something.

While Wilhelm and Etta ordered coffee inside the store, Annie disappeared into the bathroom.

Just the faintest tinge, but it was here—her period.

Ruefully, Annie wondered if all the excitement with Kjartan

had awakened the process prematurely. In any case, it was here and she had to deal with it.

A quick scan of the shelves proved comforting. She recognized several of the brands, although she didn't see her own. She selected a box and was prepared to carry it to the counter when she saw something else.

Smokkar. Condoms.

Here is a test, Annie thought, like one of those quizzes in a women's magazine designed to reveal the nuances of your personality. *"Are You an Optimist or a Pessimist?"* At that moment, Annie truly didn't know.

"A visit from your neighbor?" Etta boomed.

Annie's eyes jerked from the rack of condoms. "What?"

Etta pointed to the box of tampons.

"Oh...yes." Annie took a step forward, hoping to divert Etta's attention, but the sly crone was too fast.

"Ah, yes," Etta said, eyeing the condoms. *"Das ist gut."*

Annie recoiled at Etta's smile. "Let's go," she insisted. She laced her arm through Etta's, the way Sophie liked to do.

Big mistake, Annie thought as they left the store. I should have stayed home in bed. An entire day of winks and smiles and hints at the blossoming love affair was just the salt she needed for her wound.

Better yet, here was Kjartan's van pulling in.

Boots, jeans, red fleece jacket. Silky brown hair poking out from under her blue fleece cap. Cheeks reddened from the cold. So pretty.

So angry.

He greeted Etta and Wilhelm. Then he faced her smoky green eyes.

"Annie."

"Good morning." Her mouth was tight.

"We're off to Breidafjordur," Etta announced. "Would you like to come?"

"Can't. Busy day." He glanced toward Annie, saw her looking elsewhere.

"You should have told us you needed something," Wilhelm said, nodding toward the store. "We would have brought it back."

"No, it's no problem. I only need a few things, and the van needs gas." Annie still looked away. "Okay, I'll see you later. Have a good day."

Annie turned at that, scoffed. Kjartan met her eyes. "See you," he repeated.

An awkward pause.

"Oh!" Wilhelm slapped his forehead theatrically. "I forgot the cheese. I'll come with you." He followed Kjartan into the store.

Annie watched the two men from the back, Wilhelm with his long white hair, Kjartan with his short tousled blond. She had laced her fingers through that yellow brown hair, pulled back Kjartan's head, kissed him hungrily. Or was that only a dream?

Etta was unusually subdued. "A fight?"

"No." Reluctantly, Annie stowed the vivid memory of that kiss. "A misunderstanding."

"Hm." Etta squinted into the heavens, either checking the weather or searching for inspiration—Annie couldn't decipher which. "Just a moment," Etta said. She went to Kjartan's van and searched for something in his glove compartment.

The wind had picked up. Annie drew her fleece gloves from her pocket and pulled them on. She snugged her hat lower over her ears and flipped up the collar of her jacket.

"Why doesn't anyone here wear hats?" she asked when Etta returned. "How come I'm the only one who's ever freezing?"

Etta shrugged. "You grow accustomed to it. Always by the time we leave here I swear my blood is hotter." She leveled her gaze on Annie. "I want to tell you something. You should listen to me."

Reluctantly, Annie answered, "All right..."

"Our holiday is almost over. Wilhelm and I will be leaving on Friday. Usually by now I am so anxious to go home I could cry. But I tell you something: Not this time. Do you know why?"

"No."

"Because of you."

Annie laughed cynically. "Why's that?"

"Because I think you are right for Kjartan, and I don't want to leave until I see it." Etta held up her hand. "Uhp-buhp- buhp— you said you would listen to me."

Annie's cheeks were aflame. "It's not going to happen, " she told Etta sternly. "You can stop right now."

"It can happen. I know this man. I know how he is."

"How's that?"

"Stubborn. Stupid."

Annie smiled a little, despite her irritation. "Well, who wouldn't want to be with someone like that?"

"But he is also loyal and kind and *wunderbar*. He is a man who loves with all his heart. Marta leaving..." Etta clicked her tongue. "She was the wrong woman. I knew that the first summer I saw them together. But, as you know," Etta grinned in self-awareness, "I don't interfere in people's lives."

"Right."

"In the time we came here, Marta's parents became our friends. After they sold the farm, we wouldn't have continued coming if we didn't like Kjartan. There are many other places in Iceland like this—we could have stayed anywhere. But I tell you something that Kjartan does not know: He is like a son to me now. He would hate me to say it, but it's true. Every year we come here and I see he has lost more of his heart. But now I see how he looks at you—"

Kjartan and Wilhelm exited the store. Annie spoke quickly.

"If you had seen him look at me yesterday, you wouldn't say that."

"He is hard to understand sometimes," Etta agreed.

The men joined them.

"Okay," Kjartan said, his eyes flitting toward Annie, "I'll see you." He turned and headed for the van.

A moment later, Icelandic curses filled the parking lot. Kjartan pressed his face against the driver-side window and slapped his palm against the door.

"What's wrong?" Wilhelm asked.

Kjartan pointed through the windshield. "My keys. I locked them inside."

Annie glared at Etta. The old woman feigned innocence.

"You locked your car?" Wilhelm said. "Why did lock your car?"

"I don't know! I've never done that before."

"We'll go get another key," Etta said brightly. "Where can we find it?"

Before Annie knew what was happening, Etta and Wilhelm had slipped back into their car and started the motor.

"Wait! I'll come with you."

Wilhelm laughed cheerfully. "Not necessary! We will be back soon."

Soon? Annie thought. It would take them at least an hour. She watched helplessly as the car pulled onto the road.

She had never seen Kjartan blush before.

"Stupid," he scolded himself.

And stubborn, Annie thought—at least that's what Etta said.

Kjartan moaned in frustration. Annie listened with some amusement while Kjartan cursed himself in his lyrical native tongue. She kept a polite distance from him, bouncing her grocery bag absent-mindedly against her knee. She was glad now she'd paid the extra few *krona* for a thick plastic bag to hide her treasure.

The wind cut through her jeans, then right through her long johns. She didn't intend to stand in the open for the next hour, yet she wasn't quite ready to leave Kjartan and go inside. She idled to the concrete slab in front of the store, picked her spot along the wall, and sat down. She dropped the bag beside her.

It was the same spot, or close to it, where she had sat on her carry-on bag just four days before. Four days. How could it be so few?

Without a word, Kjartan sat down beside her. Annie felt her heart pump. Kjartan leaned back against the wall and stared out at the road.

"This is where I found you," he said matter-of-factly.

"Yep."

A long silence ensued.

Annie's heart knocked against her chest. She was certain Kjartan could hear it. She hated how little control she had over herself. She sat with her knees drawn up, her arms crossed over her chest, hoping to muffle the sound.

Kjartan sat at least a few inches away, but she could have sworn they touched. A heat field radiated from both of them.

The warmth spreading through Annie had only a little to do with being out of the wind.

Then somehow, without her noticing, Kjartan closed the distance between them. He kept his hands pressed between his knees, but he rested his arm and thigh against hers—so lightly, she might have thought it was unintentional.

Annie sighed unhappily. "What do you want?"

"I'm sorry."

"Yeah, well…" Her voice was sterner than she felt. Her mouth was dry. She barely breathed for fear of losing this tenuous touch.

"Do you want me to explain?" Kjartan offered.

"No."

Kjartan breathed deeply and relaxed. He leaned more solidly against her. Annie breathed again, too. Obviously he wasn't going to move away.

"I'm just so…embarrassed," Annie said. She couldn't look him in the eye.

Kjartan's voice was tender. "Why?"

Annie shrugged. She was in dangerous territory now. She had been known to cry.

"Oh, Annie." Kjartan reached for her gloved fingers. He lifted her hand and pressed both of theirs between his knees. "Don't say that."

Her eyes were moist. Damn. Annie cleared her throat to warn the tears away.

Kjartan interlaced his fingers more firmly in hers. He drew her in closer. "I don't know what to do," he admitted.

It wasn't what she had expected. Her voice was shakier than she liked. "Do about what?"

"Do you think I follow women to their cottages?"

Annie leaned into him more. "I don't know."

"You don't know," he repeated wryly. "Do you think I have done anything these past few days but think about you?"

Annie allowed herself a hint of a smile.

Kjartan reached for her chin and turned her to face him. He examined her heart through her eyes. Then he parted his lips and pressed them to hers.

Annie relished the taste of his lips, his tongue. She felt his warm, steady breath. It was all too much—this daze of attraction that chased away all rational thought.

A car pulled up to the gas pump. Annie barely heard it—didn't want to care—but Kjartan pulled back. He kept her hand wrapped in his own. "Óskar," Kjartan said, nodding to the stout blond man.

Óskar regarded them with amused curiosity. "Kjartan."

The conversation died there. The man at the pump stared at them openly, while Kjartan held steadily to Annie's hand.

"Bless," the man said. It was the Icelanders' standard "good-bye," but Annie preferred to think of it as literal, and directed at them personally.

When Óskar pulled away, Kjartan chuckled softly. "We'll see this in the newspapers tomorrow."

"Why? Don't people hold hands here?"

"But I was kissing you. And to see me kissing a woman—especially one that no one knows— *já*, that is unusual."

Kjartan rested his head against Annie's. "I'm sorry about yesterday. I know you were angry."

Annie didn't answer.

"I hoped you would come on the ride with me so we could talk."

"I didn't see the point. You acted like you thought you'd made a mistake."

"No. That's not what I think." Kjartan groaned. He leaned his head back against the wall. "I don't know what to do about you."

Annie squeezed his fingers. "What are your choices?"

"Fall in love with you—"

Annie's pulse shot up like a missile.

"—forget you, charge you more money so you'll leave..."

That same lethargy she felt the first time Kjartan kissed her seeped through Annie's bones once more. She recognized it as the anesthesia of emotions she didn't feel strong enough to bear. This time she wouldn't shrink away from them. If life were a composition of moments, she intended to let this one carry her forward to the next.

It's what Freydis would do.

"I think you should spend time with me," Annie said.

"I think so, too." Kjartan turned his face just enough that he could whisper in her ear. "Please, come to my bed tonight."

Annie closed her eyes and rested her head against his. "I can't. I'm..." She flashed open her bag and showed him the box. "...ineligible." She smiled shyly. "Sorry."

"Come sleep with me tonight—nothing else. I want to fall asleep with you beside me."

It was just what she wanted to hear. "All right. I will."

She couldn't imagine leaving that spot, tearing her hand away from Kjartan's, standing once more in the cold wind, but when Etta and Wilhelm returned she had no other choice.

Kjartan opened the van with his spare key. He signaled Annie to join him out of sight of the Germans.

Kjartan kissed her again sweetly. He held both of her hands. "When will you come back?"

"I don't know. It's up to Wilhelm."

"I'm leaving early tonight—five o'clock—but I'll be back early. Will you wait for me?"

Annie leaned against the van and courted another kiss. "Where? In the cottage?"

"In my bed," Kjartan answered. "Choose whichever side you like."

Annie brushed her lips against his cheek. "Let's not think for a while," she whispered, wanting to convince herself as much as him. "For now, let's just do."

Kjartan kissed her once more and turned her over to her escorts.

Annie opened the car door and floated onto the seat. She heard Kjartan call her name. She rolled down her window.

"Where you're going—Breidafjördur—that's where *Laxdaela Saga* is from. Kjartan and Gudrún. Now you will see it yourself."

Wilhelm turned to toward the back seat. "Ready?"

Etta waited until they were on the road before she turned toward Annie and threw her an inquisitive look.

Annie couldn't hide her smile.

"*Alles wird gut,*" Etta commended herself. She turned back around. "I am a very smart woman."

10

The sea air was bracing. Annie removed her jeans in the car and pulled on her rain pants, reasoning that they would provide a better windbreak. She zipped on her blue raincoat and joined Etta and Wilhelm on the shore.

"My friend isn't here," Wilhelm observed. "That's okay!" He stomped happily toward the trunk of the car and began assembling his gear.

Etta said, "Thank God you're here. I might have pushed him into the ocean this time."

They set up folding chairs near the farmhouse on the property. Wilhelm's friend used the place as a summer home. The doors were padlocked shut, the windows boarded. A loose plank creaked in the wind.

Annie pulled her hood over her fleece hat. She buried her gloved hands in the pockets of her raincoat. She knew the weather had turned objectively cold, because Etta donned a ratty gray cap to match her ratty knit sweater. After nearly five weeks away from home, Annie imagined fashion was not a priority.

Nor was it for her. Even at home she was a jeans and T-shirt devotee. She owned one pair of high heels and two fancy dresses. If anyone wanted more, Annie rationalized, they should have invited someone else.

"So," Etta began her interrogation, "things went well?"

Annie smiled indulgently. "Yes. We'll see."

"I leave on Friday," Etta reminded her.

Five days away.

"What is it you expect to see before you leave?" Annie asked.

Etta assembled her list. She made a great display of mumbling in German and counting on her fingers and looking to the heavens for verification. Finally, she said, "Love."

Annie chuckled. "And what will that look like to you?"

"I will tell you when I see it."

Annie relaxed into the chair and looked out over the bay. Wilhelm stood casting from the rocks. Beyond, she could see dozens of tiny islands colored black and bright green, just like the lava field on her ride. Sea birds circled the waves, competing for Wilhelm's prey.

"He will not catch anything there," Etta predicted, "but he doesn't care. His arm moves like that in his sleep. He can't stop."

"Does he fish at home?"

Etta rolled her eyes. "In the bathtub if he could. Yes, but not the way he can on holiday. He lives for these weeks in Iceland. He would like to live here all summer if he could."

"Do you ever think about it?"

"Sometimes, yes. Have you?"

"What?"

"Thought about living here."

Annie wasn't ready to reveal the depths of her fantasies. "No, not really."

"You should. What will you do if Kjartan is in love with you?"

"Etta, I don't think it's good to talk like this."

Etta chortled. "Why not?"

"Because...I'm very impressionable. Do you know that word?"

"Yes, I know that word."

"I sometimes have a hard time remembering which things are real, and which I've seen in a movie or read in a book."

"Kjartan isn't in a book."

"No, but this kind of thing—woman goes on vacation to Iceland, falls in love, lives happily ever after—that's definitely movie material, not real life."

Etta was not easily thwarted. "You could teach at the school."

"Maybe, maybe not. I don't know anything about that."

"I do. I know they need a teacher before September. You could teach the older students—the ones who know English."

The thought had occurred to Annie. "I don't want to play this anymore," she said. "Let's talk about something else."

"Do you want children?"

"Etta!"

"He is like a son to me. I want to know if I will have grandbabies."

Annie didn't know whether to be amused or annoyed. She settled for both. "Why do you think you can get away with this?"

"Because I am old and wise," Etta answered, shaking her finger like one of the witches from Macbeth, "and I always speak the truth."

Annie sighed, resigned. "*If* Kjartan and I ever got together, and *if* we got married one day—" Annie groaned at her own gullibility. "—then yes, maybe, if he wanted them and I wanted them...Etta, really, I don't want to play like this." Annie lost her indulgent smile. "Really." She gathered her coat in closer and pulled the hood tighter, then slouched down in her chair.

Etta patted her arm. "All right, I'll stop asking you questions. I will ask Kjartan instead."

"Don't you dare!"

Etta smiled mischievously. "If I did, would you want to know the answers?"

"No. I'll ask him my—" Annie realized she had fallen into Etta's trap.

"So you have thought about it."

Annie was already on her feet. "I promised Wilhelm I'd fish with him. Would you like me to bring you your book?"

She realized afterwards she'd barely noticed any of the landscape.

If someone had told her at the beginning of her trip that she would walk where saga heroes had walked, she would have been all eyes, taking it all in.

But she no longer dreamed of the ancient sagas. Her only interest was in the present.

They arrived home past 5:00, so Kjartan was already gone. Annie faked her way through dinner, pretending to hear what people were saying. Her mind could hold only one thought: What happens now?

Etta poached the rock fish Wilhelm had caught. The three of them ate alone. By 7:00 Annie was happy to leave them behind for a few hours of quiet and solitude.

At 9:00 she took a shower and dressed in her red flannel pajamas. The top was long-sleeved with a v-neck, the bottoms were boxers. She pulled her sweatpants over them and donned her fleece and rain coats. Then she ducked into the rain and picked her happy course toward the house.

She opened the door, removed her boots, hung her raincoat on a peg, and was just about to remove her fleece when a door downstairs creaked open.

"Kjartan?" a voice called.

She had forgotten about Petra.

Annie quickly closed her coat over her pajamas. "Uh, no, it's me—Annie."

Petra emerged from her bedroom wearing a thin white night-gown. "Yes?"

"Uh, I wanted to use the computer."

"Okay." Petra stood waiting. When Annie didn't move, she added, "You know where it is, right?"

"Yes. Um..."

Why am I so nervous? Annie thought. I have the right to be here. "Kjartan said I could use the one upstairs."

Petra seemed skeptical.

Annie began climbing the stairs.

"You can leave your coat here."

"No, that's okay. I'm cold." And I'm wearing pajamas, Annie thought.

She continued climbing without looking back. Her heart thumped as though she were cracking a safe. "Good night."

"Good night." Petra's door creaked closed.

Once in the safety of Kjartan's room, Annie relaxed. She hung up her coat and turned on the computer.

There was a long response from Shannon, three pieces of

junk mail, a short note from one of her brothers asking about plans for the holidays.

She saved the letter from Shannon for last.

RE: Your little heart.

Dear my cousin:

You owe me a new suit. I had a cup of coffee in my hands when I started reading your e-mail, and I was so shocked I dumped it all over my lap. Skinny-dipping? What would our mothers think? Making out with a burly Icelander? Who are you?

I only have a second here because clients are waiting in the lobby (I'm sure they'll appreciate the smell of coffee and wet wool during our meeting), but here's the scoop: You HAVE to let this happen—whatever "it" is. You know I don't generally advocate risk-taking and shots in the dark (ha!), but this time is different. I would SO love to see you in love. I don't care if it's just for a day. You said your little heart wants him to love you—good. If he says that he does, don't mess it up, okay? Don't worry about figuring out how to make it work. That's what's known in my business as 'the problem of step two.' You're at step one. Stay there and enjoy it.

Gotta go. I love you, I miss you, don't do anything stupid. I mean that this time! xxoo S

Smiling, Annie began her reply.

Dear my lawyer:

Please believe me when I say that what I'm about to ask you has nothing to do with what's going on here (which we'll get to shortly).

I keep looking at this contract my principal sent me, and every time I do, my stomach hurts. Shan, I don't want to go back. I knew that a few days ago when I first saw his e-mail. It's totally reckless of me to want to quit without having something else lined up, but the thought of going back to that school just makes me cold. I'll admit that part of it is the whole Mark thing, but there's a lot more to it. I'm burnt out there. I'm not getting the honors classes I asked for, and the whole place is starting to depress me. I've been feeling that way for a while—since about the Spring—but I never really considered doing anything about it.

Now that I have to keep looking at this e-mail in my inbox, it's really starting to become clear. So here's my question, Cousin Lawyer: Can I quit? (We'll get to the "should I" part in a minute.) I told my principal in May that I'd be renewing. The semester starts in late August. I'm only giving him about a month to find a replacement. Am I in trouble if I do this? Help! Be honest—don't just tell me what you think I want to hear.

As for the "should I," I don't know. You can advise me on this one, too. I'd be out of a job for at least a semester, although I suppose I could substitute teach for a while just to keep some money coming in. And then what? Come hang out with you? See if I can stand a winter there and maybe think about moving? I know this isn't like me at all, but as you can probably tell, this trip has done strange things to me. Right now all I know is what I don't want—to go back to teaching at that school—but I don't really have "the problem of step 2" worked out.

This is where you get to say, "Intervention. You're losing it." If you think I'm nuts, say so. I'm isolated in my fantasy world here, and may not be thinking straight.

As for K, things were rocky for a minute, but they seem to be back on track. I really, REALLY like him (sounds so junior high, but I have a huge crush on him). I'm sitting here in his bedroom right now wearing my pajamas, waiting for him to come home from a ride. Aunt Ruby has accompanied me to Iceland, so there won't be any action for a while, but I think that's good. Slow things down and see what's what.

I'm almost afraid to say this because I know you'll run with it, but here it is: I'm almost in love with him. I barely know him—I've only been here five days, and one of them I spent sleeping—so I have no business feeling this way. But I think I do. So there you have it. I'm confessing it to my lawyer. Keep it confidential.

Sorry about your suit. Send me the cleaning bill. Right now I can only pay it in Icelandic krona, but I'll get it to you.

Thank you for loving me and missing me. Same here.

Don't do anything stupid (like fall in love with a stranger). xxoo A.

She had just pushed the send key when she heard the door downstairs close. Warmth spread from her heart to the tips of her fingers and toes. Her smile was immediate.

Putting it into words—"I'm almost in love with him"—felt

better than she expected. She thought she would be afraid to see it on the page. But it looked right, felt right.

Kjartan opened his bedroom door and came straight for her. "I saw your boots downstairs," he said, reaching over the chair to hug her the way she had seen Guy do to Sophie the first night she met them. Like Sophie, she reached back and wrapped her arms around Kjartan's waist. He rested his chin on the top of her head.

"Writing?"

"Mm-hm." She closed out the program and stood to give him a better hug. "Good ride?"

"I don't know. I don't remember any of it. I was already thinking of this." He kissed her long and sweetly, his tongue flicking softly against hers.

Annie breathed in the scent of him—sweat and wet horse. She ran her hands along his back, feeling the strength.

"I saw Petra downstairs," Annie said.

"Hm, yes, I forgot to say something to you about that."

"Is there a problem?"

"No. I didn't want you to be surprised when you saw her."

"I guess I knew she lived here, but I never really thought about it. She seemed pretty surprised to see me—especially when I headed upstairs to your room."

"What did you tell her?"

"That I was going to use your computer—which I did." Annie leaned back and studied his face critically.

"What?" he asked, smiling.

"You don't have to tell me this if you don't want, but I'm going to ask anyway. Was there ever anything between you and Petra?"

"*Nei.* Never." Kjartan reached back and withdrew Annie's hands from around his waist. Still holding onto them he leaned forward and kissed her. "I'm going to take a shower. Do you need anything?"

Annie shook her head.

Kjartan tugged at the waistband of her sweatpants. "Is this what you sleep in?"

"*Nei,*" Annie answered. "You'll see."

As he kissed her cheek Kjartan cupped one hand over the red flannel covering her breast. "Is this what you sleep in?"

"If you're going to make this hard for me," Annie teased, "maybe I shouldn't stay."

"It will be harder for me, but I want you to stay."

As soon as she heard the shower running, Annie slipped out of her sweatpants. She kept on her socks for warmth until Kjartan came to bed.

She pulled down the covers on one of the twin beds and climbed in. Just to make abundantly clear she did not intend to sleep alone in the same room with him, she untucked the covers on his side as well, and did her best to make it all one bed.

She had just settled back onto her pillow when the door to Kjartan's bedroom opened.

Annie couldn't say who was more alarmed: herself or the redhead.

11

Petra's face went dead. "Oh." She stood with one foot in the room, her thin white nightgown revealing her anticipation.

Annie pulled the covers up to her chin, as though she were in a 1940's movie. What could she say? "Hi!"? "Thanks for letting me use the computer—I saw something else I liked"? She said nothing. She might have peeped in surprise, but she wasn't sure.

Petra glanced toward Kjartan's bathroom. With one more penetrating look at Annie, she stepped back and closed the door.

Annie let out her breath. Questions raced into her mind. She didn't know whether to bound out of bed instantly and retreat to the cottage, or wait and let Kjartan explain. She did not—*not*—want to play this part. If Kjartan and Petra were a couple—if Petra had reason to think they were a couple—Annie would not interfere. She would not be the Miss Biology in this threesome—there was no justice in that.

Kjartan came out of the bathroom toweling off his hair. It stuck out from his head like the bushy blond forelock on his favorite horse. He wore a pale gray T-shirt and the blue scrubs Annie had seen him in the other night. He looked as handsome as she had ever seen him.

Petra would have thought so, too.

"Annie? What's wrong?"

In as calm a voice as she could muster, she said, "You had a visitor."

Kjartan glanced toward the door and gave an angry sigh. "I'm sorry."

"Should I leave?"

"No! Why would you ask that?"

"Because," Annie whispered, hoping Kjartan would do the same, "obviously she thought you had other plans tonight."

"Annie..." Kjartan crossed the room and sat on top of the covers beside her. He reached for her hand. "Annie, listen to me. I have nothing with Petra. She only works for me."

"Have you ever had anything with her?"

"No."

"Then why would she come up here in her nightgown? Why would she come in while you're in the shower?"

"She probably wanted to ask me what we are doing tomorrow."

Annie had no doubt Petra wanted to do more than talk about the schedule. What she didn't know was whether Kjartan were concealing something, or were simply naive.

"Petra sometimes...I think she wishes I would..." Kjartan paused, cleared his throat. Annie wondered if he were uncomfortable sullying another woman's reputation by admitting she had thrown herself at him. "I already decided not to ask her work here after this summer. I decided that before you came."

Annie kept her eyes on the red plaid bedcover. "Okay..."

Kjartan squeezed her hand. "Annie, look at me."

She did. And seeing his expression—both sincere and tender—she knew she would believe him, whatever he was about to say.

"You are the first...I have not asked a woman to my bed for a long time. I have not..." He hesitated, as though deciding how much to confess. Annie already suspected the truth. "I have not made love to a woman since Marta. You shouldn't worry about Petra—or any other woman."

He raised her hand to his lips and kissed the center of her palm. Heat spread through her torso. "I'm glad you're here tonight," Kjartan said. "I've been thinking about it all day."

"Me, too."

He rose from the bed, strode to the door, and turned the lock. "I'm sorry that happened. I want you to be comfortable here."

He returned to the bathroom, brushed his teeth, then flicked off the light and came to bed.

He breached the divide between the mattresses and pulled her in close. Annie stretched out against his body and let him kiss away the last of her tension.

Kjartan's hand drifted down her back, rounded over her rump, and found the hem of her flannel boxers. He continued his course, running his rough, dry fingers across the back of her thigh. Annie sighed and moved in closer. She fervently wished she were eligible for more that night, but her period had its own wicked sense of humor.

The more he explored her body—even from the outside of her clothes—the more aroused Annie felt him become. "Would you like me to help you with that?" she offered.

Kjartan sighed. He wrapped his arms around Annie and nestled her from behind. "No," he answered, "I want to wait for you."

The crack between the beds threatened to suck them both to the floor, but Kjartan didn't seem concerned. Annie scooted back further so they were both poised on Kjartan's half of the bed.

His excitement had not abated. Annie couldn't resist rubbing against him.

He groaned and moved his hips back. "I can wait."

Annie whispered, "I can't."

"Sshhh." Kjartan wrapped his arms more tightly around her and rested his face against her neck. "*Góda nótt*, Annie—good night. Thank you for being here."

"Good night." She almost said more—felt ready to say more—but like Kjartan, she would practice patience.

Four days to wait—five days at most. She wondered how she would last that long.

PETRA STOOD in the cafeteria kitchen, sullenly smoking a cigarette. Annie glanced away quickly and concentrated on the coffee pot.

A new group of travelers milled about. They were mostly adults, with a few teens. She couldn't identify their language.

Sophie kissed her friend on the cheek. "Do you know we are leaving tomorrow?"

"What? No!"

"Yes, I'm sorry." Sophie refilled her cup and drizzled in cream.

Petra's smoke drifted over them. Annie was determined not to look her way.

While Annie loaded her plate, Sophie explained. "Guy has to go back to work this weekend. And I am beginning school again soon."

"What's medical school like?"

Sophie seemed perplexed. "I don't know. Why do you ask me?"

"Etta told me you were going to be a doctor."

"Ah, Etta." Sophie shook her head. "She has such big dreams for us."

"So you're not going to be a doctor."

"I don't know, perhaps one day. I like the idea of it, but now I am in school to learn massage."

"Oh." The occupation seemed a good fit, and Annie said so. "But why would Etta tell me—"

Sophie shrugged. "Why does she tell me you will marry Kjartan?"

Annie stammered, "She tells you that?"

"Since you arrived. She likes to pretend she knows the future." Sophie glanced toward the table, where Etta was engaged in friendly bickering with her husband. "She told me Guy will propose marriage before we leave Iceland, so I suppose we will see?"

They joined the Germans and Guy. Sophie pulled her chair up closer to her boyfriend's and laid her head on his shoulder. Guy whispered something and kissed her. Both young lovers smiled with contentment. Annie smiled in empathy, feeling some of that same contentment herself.

"Can you believe," Etta asked the group, "that Wilhelm will not take me to Reykjavik? He wants to spend every last minute here."

"Why should you go to Reykjavik?" Sophie asked, winking at Wilhelm. "The fishing is much better here."

"Exactly!" Wilhelm agreed.

Etta rolled her eyes.

"What's in Reykjavik?" Annie asked.

"Plays, culture, food—"

"I will take you to a play in Stuttgart," Wilhelm promised.

Etta pointed to Annie. "I am going to tell Kjartan he must take you to Reykjavik sometimes. You should go to the city—"

"Sshh! Etta, don't—" Annie dared not look behind her toward the kitchen. She knew how well Etta's voice carried.

"Why? We're all friends here."

Annie leaned across the table and whispered to Etta, "Please, don't say any more."

Etta shrugged, miffed. Annie would have to appease her later. For now, she wanted to eat in peace without feeling Petra's hot glare scorching her back.

"We should ride twice today," Sophie proposed.

"Yes," Annie said, "I think we should."

"Petra is taking out a group at eleven."

Annie kept her expression neutral. Kjartan had already told her his schedule for the day. "There's another group at noon, I think. Could we go with them instead?"

"Of course." Sophie looked to Guy for confirmation.

"And then tonight?" Guy asked.

Annie knew that answer as well. "Six o'clock. There's a group coming from Akureyri. Kjartan's taking them on a three-hour ride."

Sophie's smile was sly. "You know so much."

Annie flushed. She glanced at Etta, who seemed to accept the blush as an apology.

"Of course she knows," Etta said. "And so she should."

Shortly before noon Annie met up with the other riders inside the stable. Kjartan was busy helping one of the clients find an appropriate-fitting cap. He spared an instant to exchange a look with Annie, then went back to work.

Annie joined Sophie beside the Frenchwoman's favorite

horse, the gray gelding with the salt and pepper mane. "I will miss him," Sophie cooed. "He has been so good to me."

Annie still had no preference among the herd. She trusted Kjartan to choose one for her.

"Annie," Sophie said, stroking the gelding's forehead, "you should be careful with Etta."

"Yes," Annie sighed, "I know."

"She sometimes goes too far. I think she will go as far as you allow her. I heard her talk to Kjartan this morning, after breakfast. I don't know if you will like that."

"Talk to him about what?"

"What she said at breakfast—that he should take you to Reykjavik."

Annie felt a cold dread. She didn't want Kjartan pushed. She didn't even know herself how far she should take things.

"What did he say?"

"Mm, nothing, just 'okay,' I think."

Annie held her irritation in check. For all the good that woman did—Annie had to admit the ploy of locking Kjartan's keys in the van had worked to her advantage—she seemed to do an equal amount of harm. No one had the right to say half the things Etta felt entitled to say.

"I like her," Sophie added, "but I'm careful with her, you know? I would not like her saying something to Guy."

How do you know she hasn't? Annie thought.

Sophie seemed to read her mind. "He would tell me," she said. "We don't have secrets."

Kjartan matched the seven riders to their mounts. He directed Annie to a chestnut gelding. "That's Fossi. You'll like him." Kjartan brushed against Annie's arm with a subtlety she admired. Her skin prickled.

Sophie led the group. Annie followed in second position. She glanced back at Kjartan, who in Petra's absence had tethered his horse to a beginner's.

Annie turned back around, enjoying the memory of that first ride with Kjartan. She couldn't have known then how spending six hours tied together would hasten their romance.

"I have taken this ride before," Sophie said. "We will go over this hill onto some rocks, then along a river until we come to the sea."

Annie watched Sophie's long braid stutter against her back. Both horses were in *tölt*, and glided along at an easy pace.

The trail opened up to a long grassy flat. Sophie's horse increased his speed.

"Don't follow me!" Sophie called over her shoulder. "He is going too fast!" The horse rocketed into a gallop.

But Annie had no choice. The chestnut raced after Sophie, his hooves eating up the turf.

"Sophie!"

Annie pulled as forcefully as she could on the reins. The horse jerked his head and sped on. Annie leaned forward, clutching her legs to the horse's side, praying that she wouldn't fall.

She stared down at the horse's churning hooves, at the grass disappearing beneath them. She lost all sense of time. She was trapped in this horror, terrified beyond reason, unable to think of a single thing she could do to help herself.

Where was Sophie? Couldn't she see what was happening? Wouldn't she have stopped by now?

Annie dared to lift her head and look out in front of them. Sophie was still ahead, still bounding over the flat.

Annie felt ill. Fear overcame her. The grass looked so soft.... This ride was too hard.... The grass would break her fall....

She slipped from Fossi's back, barely rolling out of range of his hooves. She lay there, not knowing whether she was hurt or dead or dreaming.

An hour later, or maybe a minute, or maybe an eternity...

"Annie? Annie?"

It was Kjartan. Dear Kjartan...

"Annie." He said it more sternly this time. She had to open her eyes.

The sky over him was so blue. Was that the ocean she heard, or the mad echoing of her horse's hooves? No, it was Sophie's horse, Annie saw, thundering back to the group.

"Are you hurt?" Kjartan asked. His forehead creased in

concern. Gently he tested her arms. He ran his hands over her legs. Just like the night before...

Sophie was in tears. "I couldn't stop! He wouldn't listen! I'm so sorry! Annie!" She held Annie's hand between her own. "Are you all right? Are you hurt?"

"I'm okay," Annie answered, feeling now that it was true. Slowly, with Kjartan's help, she sat up.

Now Annie cried, too, a brief cloudburst to relieve her tension. She was all right. It was over.

The other riders stood nervously at a distance, mumbling to each other. A miraculous feat, Annie thought wryly, since only a few of them spoke the same language.

Feeling the stiffness already setting in, Annie managed to rise from the ground.

"You're all right?" Kjartan repeated. He sounded tense, gruff. "Take a moment. Tell me."

Annie nodded, a little confused by his tone. "I'm okay."

Kjartan looked back at the other riders. Then he turned to Sophie.

"Can you take her back?"

Annie gaped at him. "You're going on?"

"I have to," he said simply. "I have other customers."

Annie glared in disbelief.

"I'll take her," Sophie said. "Don't worry."

Kjartan confounded Annie further by kissing her lightly on the side of her mouth.

"I'm sorry, Annie. I wish I could take you home. If Petra was here I could."

"It's fine," she answered dully. "Just go."

Kjartan reached for her hand. Annie moved it out of range.

"Thank you," he said to Sophie. The young woman nodded. Then Kjartan returned to the group.

Annie's eyes misted.

"He really can't leave them," Sophie said.

"He could. He doesn't want to."

Had she made a mistake again? How many times was she going to fall for this same man and then watch him pull away? When was she going to learn?

Sophie retrieved their two horses from the rider who held their reins. She led them back to Annie.

"We can walk," Sophie said. "Or we can ride when you're ready."

"I don't think I'll ever be ready," Annie said, her voice thick. "Let's walk."

After a slow, painful retreat to the cottage, Annie examined the bruise. It covered her left leg from the hip to the knee. Another one bloomed where her knees had crashed together.

"Does this hurt?" Sophie asked, manipulating Annie's shoulder.

"Ugh. Yes."

"Here, lie down."

Annie stretched out face down on her bed. Sophie helped her remove her shirt and bra, then she covered Annie with a blanket.

"Do you have any lotion?"

"There's some in the bathroom."

Sophie returned, rubbing her hands together to heat them. She laid them gently on Annie's shoulders and began to massage.

Sophie's touch was both painful and restorative—a pain Annie came to appreciate, like biting into a hot chili pepper. The deeper Sophie's strokes, the harder the pressure, the more good Annie knew she was doing.

"You're very good at this," Annie mumbled.

"*Merci.* Sshh...relax..."

Annie awoke to a different set of hands. And to kisses across her shoulders.

Kjartan knelt beside her bed. "Annie, I'm so sorry."

She turned her face to the wall. "I doubt it."

"Annie..." He kissed the back of her head, then resumed the massage that had awakened her.

His hands were rough but warm, and he seemed to know just where she hurt. The fall had twisted her in ways she hadn't felt at the time, and now every muscle ached.

He worked his fingers deeply into the knots in her neck. His thumbs kneaded the base of her skull. When he pressed his knuckles deeply into the tops of her shoulders, Annie couldn't help but moan. The sensation was rich—both excruciating and exquisite. She marveled at how intuitively his fingers moved, finding every secret hurt and coaxing it to the surface.

Kjartan folded the blanket down, exposing her bare back. Annie tensed, acutely aware that she wore only a pair of underwear. But Kjartan didn't seem bent on seduction. He worked with the same professional detachment Sophie had displayed, going after the spots that made her flinch, working deeply or lightly as the muscles demanded.

She wanted his touch—wanted him there—but she couldn't forget the cold efficiency with which he'd dispatched her back to the farm while he rode on with the others. A healing touch was no substitute for kindness when she needed it. His disloyalty stung, and no matter how contrite he might be now, she wouldn't let him forget how he had hurt her.

Still, she regretted it almost as soon as she said it.

"Did you enjoy the rest of your ride?" She hated the sound of her voice—strident, snappish—just the kind of woman she didn't want to be.

Kjartan didn't pause, didn't seem affected by her foul mood. He worked her screaming muscles slowly, deeply, thoroughly. Using the heels of his palms, he pressed outward from her spine, making her grunt with subdued pleasure. When Kjartan's fingers brushed against the sides of her breasts, Annie felt her breath catch. This was it—this was when he would try to turn it into something more. But he didn't. Kjartan moved on to some other ache, leaving Annie with a new one brewing deep inside.

He raised the blanket to her shoulders and smoothed it across her back. Then he lifted the blanket from her left hip and leg.

Annie tensed. "That hurts," she warned, even before he'd touched her. She wasn't worried about the pain—she trusted his touch. What worried her was her own reaction to feeling his hands on her bare thigh.

"Really, Kjartan, don't."

"I'll be careful."

He ran his hands expertly down the length of her thigh, testing for areas of tenderness. When she flinched, he stopped, waited for her to relax again.

How could he be so sensitive in this way, Annie wondered,

and yet treat her the way that he had? He worked gently, patiently, easing the stiffness in her hip, working the over-wrought muscles in her calves and the back of her thighs.

"How do you know how to do this?"

"I work with the horses," Kjartan answered, as though the connection should be obvious.

He covered her left leg and exposed her right. Slowly he melted her down to the bone.

When she felt his lips on her shoulders once more, she fought hard not to give in. But she was strong. She would not forgive him so easily.

He swept back her hair and kissed her cheek. If he had asked her then, "Do you feel better?" or anything similarly solicitous, she would have had a surly comeback. But he didn't ask that. Instead he said, "Come riding with me tonight."

Annie jerked her head from the pillow. "What? Are you crazy?"

"You should go riding again as soon as possible."

"Why? So you can finish the job?"

"Waiting too long will only make you more scared."

"I've been scared," Annie said. "I'm scared every time I get on a horse. I think I'm done trying to work through it." She resisted adding, "You idiot," although she was sure her tone said it for her.

Kjartan sat back on his heels. "I'm trying to help you."

"The time to help me was back there, when I was lying on the ground." Her anger threatened to bring an order of tears. Annie wouldn't let that happen this time—she fed her anger to make herself feel stronger. "What if Sophie hadn't been there today? Would you have sent me back on my own?"

"I don't know," he answered softly. "I would have decided then."

"Why did you give me that horse? I told you I don't like to go fast!" The speech wasn't going as well as she had planned. When she'd rehearsed it on the hobble home, it sang, it roared, it deci-mated. But now her voice trembled and the forecast was for tears.

"I'm sorry about Fossi. I didn't know he would do that.

Horses are hard to predict." Kjartan hesitated. He rested his hand softly on her back. "But you should have stayed on him."

"What?!" Annie clutched the blanket to her chest and grimaced as she struggled to sit up. "How can you say that?"

"I saw you roll off him. That was the worst thing you could do. If you had fallen a centimeter closer, he could have killed you."

"Thank you for the advice," she answered stiffly, but she couldn't keep the shakiness from her voice. The truth was, what he said frightened her. She didn't want to think how much worse the fall could have been. And she suspected that Kjartan was right: She should have stayed on, rather than risk tangling in the horse's hooves. But she wouldn't let him deflect the blame. He had assigned her that runaway horse. When she needed him most he had abandoned her. Not that she would accept it, but where was his apology?

Defiant, she answered, "I'll remember that if I ever lose my mind and go riding again. Do you have anything else to tell me? Did I fall on the wrong hip? Should I have rolled a different way? Maybe I should have smiled afterward so your other clients wouldn't think anything was wrong."

"Annie—" Kjartan sighed in resignation. "I care about you."

"Yeah, I can see that." Annie lay back down and turned her face to the wall.

She felt Kjartan lean over her, perhaps to kiss her, but he retreated before he made contact.

"We leave at six o'clock, if you want to go. I'll ride with you, on the tether. I promise you'll be all right."

"Your promise doesn't mean anything." She was glad he couldn't see the pain written on her face as she said it. "I don't trust you anymore."

The words were out before she could stop them. She wanted to turn to him, reach for him, tell him she didn't mean it. But at the same time she wanted him to feel the sting—to feel even a fraction of the pain she had felt that afternoon when he dismissed her and went on with his life.

She heard him stand, take his first few steps toward the door. She had ample time to take it back—wanted to, meant to—but he was out the door and she still hadn't said a word.

Victory is sweet, she thought. As sweet as poison.

Later she watched from her window while Kjartan led Sophie and Guy and two other riders onto the trail. Regret scratched at her heart. Did Freydis feel this way after she convinced those men later in her life to kill her husband? Annie doubted it. Freydis made decisions swiftly and never turned back. She knew what she wanted and she lived with her mistakes.

Annie dressed and walked to the house. In the kitchen Petra stood at the sink washing dishes. Annie nearly turned around and left, but her empty stomach emboldened her.

"Hello."

"Hello," Petra answered. "Do you want something to eat?"

Annie lowered herself gingerly into the chair. "Yes, please."

"I heard about your fall. Are you all right?"

"Yes, a little sore, but nothing too bad."

"You're lucky. It's dangerous to fall that way."

"So I heard."

Petra warmed a plate of salmon and little potatoes. She set it in front of Annie and went back to washing dishes.

Annie was grateful that Petra seemed no more inclined to make small talk than she was. She ate in silence, choking back the over-salted fish, but savoring the delicate white potatoes lightly bathed in butter.

When she finished she scraped the bones into the garbage and loaded the plate into the dishwasher. "Okay, well, good night," Annie said, aiming for the door.

"You should try the hot pool," Petra offered. "It will help you feel better tomorrow."

"That's a good idea. Thanks."

Annie felt a tug of guilt for the way she had been feeling about the redhead. Had she misread her? Or, Annie thought, had word already spread that she and Kjartan had fought? Maybe Petra could warm to her now that Annie was no longer a rival.

It was raining again. The ride wouldn't have been good anyway, she reasoned. Besides, her back ached, her leg was purpling nicely, and she couldn't imagine what it would have taken to sit astride one of those maniacal, reckless creatures again.

Still, she wished she could have ridden with Sophie one more time. And even more, she worried that she really could have mustered the courage to get back on a horse, but had passed up the chance just so she could nurture her grudge.

She had passed up more than that, she realized. After a night of unrivaled peace sleeping in Kjartan's arms, tonight she would be back in her cold, small bed, lonelier than she had ever been.

Why did he do it? How could he leave her like that? Why couldn't he put her first for once?

Annie shook her head wryly. What do you mean "for once?" she scolded herself. You act as though you've been with this man for ages.

She changed into her bathing suit and covered it with a layer of long underwear followed by her rain gear. Then she set out in the rain. As she neared the school, she heard laughter rising from the pool along with the steam. She wouldn't be alone this time, but maybe that was best. Solitude was fertile ground for brooding, and she had done enough of that.

She removed her rain clothes and long underwear and hung them on one of the few spare pegs in the women's dressing room. Other women stood naked or half-clothed, chatting in a language Annie wasn't in the mood to admire. She stepped into the shower wearing her bathing suit and soaped as best she could.

She could barely remember the giddiness of nudity a few nights before. That entire night had been so unlike her—the skinny dipping, her wild passion toward a man she barely knew. She had regained her senses now, every old modesty falling back into place: We don't undress in public. We don't kiss strange men.

She padded past the pool. The crowd seemed to be college-aged, like Sophie and Guy. Couples hung on each other in the awkward manner of new lovers. Annie wondered how many of them had discovered each other over the course of their trip, and how many would part ways once their feet hit the soils of home.

Four people crowded into the small hot pool. Annie nearly

turned back rather than squeeze among them, but her screaming muscles spurred her on. She nodded politely, received a few nods back. The four made room for her as she lowered herself into the pool.

Heaven. The heat penetrated her pain and made her forget every trouble. Annie closed her eyes and leaned her head against the rim. She gave in to the water's therapy and ceased thinking for a while. Those moments were the most peaceful she had experienced in hours.

But eventually the thoughts seeped back in, nourishing her lingering anger.

He had ruined everything. They could have been together tonight, and every night until she left, but now that fantasy was over. She was back to being a tourist, a guest. She had twelve days left of her vacation. Twelve long days. Sophie would be gone. Etta and Wilhelm were leaving in a few days. Then what? Wander around avoiding Kjartan? Strike up a friendship with Petra? Regret gnawed at Annie. Maybe, she thought, this whole thing was a mistake. Maybe she shouldn't have come alone. Maybe she shouldn't have come at all. She could have spent a few happy weeks visiting Shannon. She should have invited Shannon along.

She realized then that her vacation was over. She had had her fun, had met interesting people and seen beautiful, exotic country, but now it was time to go home. She could catch a ride to the airport on Friday from Etta and Wilhelm. Spend the rest of her vacation with Shannon. That made the most sense. She had proven she could travel alone, could master the fear that had kept her home for so long. But there was no reason to stay if it wasn't fun anymore. She owed it to herself to admit that and move on.

She would make the arrangements tonight. If she hurried, she could use Kjartan's downstairs computer before he returned. Annie rinsed in the shower, dried her bathing suit as best she could, then pulled on her clothes over it. The rain was coming harder. She was wet inside and out, but it didn't matter. She was going home. Home to steamy Minneapolis, then back to the dry heat of Arizona. Out of this incessant rain and daylight and the fog of ill-considered romance. She had lived her saga fantasy, but now it was time to resume her normal life.

By the time she returned to the farm she was thoroughly chilled. She quickly changed out of her wet clothes and into her nighttime uniform of sweats and a T-shirt. She threw on her raincoat and hurried to the house. Plane reservations would take only a few minutes. She could be safe in her cottage before the riders returned.

Out of habit she clicked on her mailbox first. Only one message.

Annie stared at the subject line for a moment, trying to put it into context. That last e-mail to Shannon seemed so long ago. So much had happened since then.

Annie's stomach burned. She was almost afraid to read the letter. But better to face her folly, she decided. She had written with such foolish hope, telling Shannon she was ready to quit her job and start another life, knowing but not saying that what she really wanted was to start a life with Kjartan.

How pathetic, Annie thought. How naive. Just one more fantasy in a lifetime of make-believe. But like Freydis, she would go forward, live with her mistakes. Annie opened the letter and read.

Subject: *"Quit."*

1 2

Sophie was uncommonly somber the next morning. She hugged Annie tightly. "You have been such a good friend. I will miss you!"

"I'm going to miss you, too. What time is your bus?"

"Eight o'clock."

"We have to leave or you'll miss it," Etta interjected. Her voice was particularly hoarse so early in the morning. She and Wilhelm leaned against their wet car, sipping coffee from steaming mugs, looking as if they'd had as little sleep as Annie had.

"I'll give you my e-mail address," Annie said. "Will you write to me?"

"Of course."

"Do you think you'll ever come to the U.S.? Maybe to Arizona?"

"I don't know," Sophie said. "Perhaps. And perhaps you will come to France?"

"Maybe, some day. Will you ever come back to Iceland, do you think?"

Sophie pursed her fine French lips. "I don't know—it's hard, you know? There are so many beautiful places to visit."

Etta checked her watch and scowled. Annie hurried to find some last, perfect words to express her fondness for the young woman. She didn't often make such quick connections with people, and so she was unaccustomed to the idea of letting them go just as easily.

She drew Sophie away from the group and whispered, "Was Etta right? About Guy?"

"That he would ask to marry me?" Sophie laughed. "No."

"Well, you're not out of Iceland yet."

"I think Etta can only be right about one thing," Sophie said. "I think you will have a very good life with Kjartan."

The pain was acute. "No, that won't happen. After yesterday...well, I've decided to leave early—on Friday, when Etta and Wilhelm go."

"But why? No, no, don't do that." Sophie swept her finger down Annie's cheek. "No, this is wrong. Annie, do not turn away from love. It comes when it comes and you must accept it. Here it has come to you."

"It hasn't come to me. You saw yesterday—"

"Yesterday was one day. And you may be angry with me, but I agree with Kjartan's decision. He was right to go on."

"How could—"

"Annie, I know how Kjartan feels. Last night he told me—"

"Ladies!" Etta called. "Sophie, we must go *now*."

Sophie hugged Annie and whispered, "Take this love from Kjartan. He is yours—believe me. Don't run away from him." Then she raced to the car and disappeared inside before Annie could tell her she was wrong.

Annie stood alone in the driveway watching the car pull away. Already she felt the loss of Sophie's bright humor and contagious smile.

She turned and limped back toward her cottage. She felt better than she had the night before, but a restless night had left her stiff again. A long, hot shower seemed the appropriate cure for all that ailed her body and heart.

Standing amidst the steam, letting the volcanic heat seep into her bones, Annie felt a strange comfort. She was really, truly alone. She knew it before, of course, but now she felt ready to wear it, like a pair of jeans that she had finally broken in. She was independent, a traveler abroad, a grown woman with no one to make decisions for her but herself.

If she wasn't having a good time, she could leave. That's what she had reminded herself the night before. No one demanded she serve out her time there. Reservations could be changed. She owed nothing to anyone.

"Don't run away," Sophie had said, but was she running away? Wasn't she just making a positive choice about how to spend her time? Even if she and Kjartan were getting along, what did that mean? She still had to leave eventually, if not this week, then next. There was no point in getting in deeper, even if that were still possible. Kjartan had simply made it easier to leave. It would never be easier to go than now, when they were at odds.

Annie hadn't changed her plane reservations the night before. Shannon's e-mail unsettled her, made her question everything she had been feeling in the past several days.

How did she feel about her job? Did she really want to go back? Back to teaching four periods of Freshman English and one of Sophomore, even though the principal had promised to move her into Honors Seniors classes? His explanation and apology made sense—seniority, budgeting issues, Annie's "talent" for teaching rowdy students who would rather be anywhere but in class—but still Annie felt the sting of disappointment. By now she should be getting the prime appointments. She had put in her time with extra duties—lunch monitor, extracurricular programs, student teacher mentoring—but none of that seemed to matter. Just one semester off while she tended to her dying mother had set her back almost to the beginning. Mr. Messinger shrugged it off, telling her he was glad he could give her that time when she needed it, but now she had to live with the consequences. Others had moved ahead. She had slipped behind. That's life, Mr. Messinger said. And Annie had swallowed it all.

By the time she got to the school, the new crop of boarders were just starting to get up. Everywhere across the gym floor and out into the halls she saw sleepy heads lifting from sleeping bags.

Two of the adult escorts were already sipping coffee in the cafeteria. Etta and Wilhelm were still not back from driving Sophie and Guy to the bus stop. Petra stood in the kitchen talking with another worker. They paused to watch Annie as she walked toward the life-giving silver coffee pot.

Annie resolved to be friendly. "Good morning."

"Good morning," Petra responded automatically. The other worker, an attractive blond woman in her mid-thirties, greeted her pleasantly.

Annie poured her first cup of coffee and took it to the far table. She sat with her back to Petra and stared out the window.

Another cloudy day. String enough of those together, she thought, and this place might seem a bit gloomy. So far Iceland's summer seemed a lot like a Tucson winter, with its low clouds and sporadic rainfall, and winds that whipped through the seams.

Scruffy teenagers were beginning to stumble into the cafeteria. Annie left her jacket hanging over her chair in the universal symbol of "dibs." She helped herself to more coffee and gathered the ingredients of her usual breakfast.

Why did he seem to take up the room? She felt him rather than saw him at first. He stood in the doorway of the cafeteria and locked eyes with her. Annie felt a quiver in her gut. She focused on her food selection and tried to keep her pulse in check.

He looked awful—bleary-eyed, stubble-faced, stooped with weariness. He came toward her, his gray wool socks scuffing across the floor.

"Hello."

Annie concentrated on the jam. "Hello."

"Can I talk to you?"

She looked up then and saw an expression that matched her own: hurt, disappointment, but lingering hope.

"All right."

He poured himself a cup a coffee and followed her back to the table. He sat across from her, propped his elbows on the table, and took a long sip of the muddy brew.

"I have something to ask."

Annie's mouth was dry. "Okay."

"What are you doing tonight?"

Annie fumbled for an answer. "Well, let's see...very busy schedule..." She pretended to take great interest in her toast.

"Will you come out with me tonight?"

"Out with you? Like on a date?"

"Yes, I suppose." Kjartan cleared his throat. "I want to take you to dinner."

His eyes were rimmed red with sleeplessness. Annie felt a surge of sympathy for him—no matter how hard her night had been, maybe his had been worse.

"Dinner? Um..." What was the harm? Call it a farewell dinner. "All right."

Kjartan took another sip of coffee. His eyes drifted toward the kitchen. "I'll be right back."

She let a little time drift by before casually looking over her shoulder. Kjartan stood with his back to her, talking to the blond kitchen worker. Petra stood to the side, her expression unreadable.

When he returned he asked, "Is six o'clock okay?"

"Um, all right, sure."

"It takes about thirty minutes to get there, so I can pick you up at five-thirty."

The whole thing had a momentum of its own. "Okay, sure."

Reality nudged her. "Wait—is it fancy? I didn't bring anything nice to wear—remember you said no formal dinners."

"It's not fancy."

"But all my clothes are filthy. I think I've managed to get every one of them wet, and nothing seems to dry here."

"You can wash clothes in my house."

"Really?" Visions of dry T-shirts danced in her head. "But what should I wear tonight?"

"What you're wearing now. I told you, it isn't fancy. It's just a nice restaurant owned by some people I know. I hope you like fish."

The truth was, after eating it every night for a week, Annie was ready for anything else—preferably something with salsa on the side.

"Sure, that's fine."

"Good." His business completed, Kjartan journeyed toward

the food table and loaded a plate. He returned with a prodigious amount of meat, cheese, black bread, and pickled fish. He sat across from her and settled into his meal.

Etta stood in the doorway, her enormous square teeth exposed by an equally gigantic smile.

"*Guten morgen,*" she said to them both. Wilhelm smiled his greeting and kept moving toward the food.

Instinctively Annie sat up straighter, looking guiltily toward Kjartan.

Kjartan didn't share her discomfort. "Good morning."

Etta pulled back the chair beside Annie and rested her elbows on the table, no less embarrassed to be observing them than Kjartan was to be observed.

"So sad to see them go," Etta croaked in her deep morning voice. "What will you do when we leave, too?" she asked Kjartan. "Will you cry, as I did?"

Kjartan raised an eyebrow. "I will have to go to bed, I'll be so sad."

Etta enlisted Annie. "He pretends not to care, but he really has a soft heart, doesn't he?"

Annie shrugged. Kjartan caught her eye. Was that amusement she saw? Some secret signal? She glanced down at her empty plate.

Wilhelm joined them with a sensible breakfast of muesli, *skyr,* and pickled herring on toast.

Etta sighed dramatically. "It is good I'm leaving before you," she told Annie. "I don't know how I would live here with both you and Sophie gone. And who knows? Maybe you won't leave at all."

Annie couldn't look at Kjartan. She wished desperately that Etta would stop talking.

"What will you do today?" Etta asked them both. Kjartan described a meeting with men from the co-op about putting up hay for the winter. He had only one group to guide, at 2:00.

"No night ride?" Etta asked.

"No, I have a date tonight, with Annie."

Etta's eyebrows lifted nearly to her hairline. Annie was tired of blushing, but here it was again.

Etta patted Annie's hand. "Good, Kjartan. Finally you take an old woman's advice."

"How do you know it wasn't my advice?" Wilhelm asked, his mouth full of herring.

Etta ignored him. "Where will you take her?"

"*Takk Fiskurs.*"

Etta nodded in approval. She winked at Annie. "A very romantic place."

It was all too much for Annie. She pushed back her chair and carried her dirty plate to the kitchen. There was Petra, giving her the same sullen look as before.

Too many people knew too much, Annie thought, and she herself knew too little. Everyone assumed things were settled between her and Kjartan, when she knew well they were anything but.

She paused at the table. "I need a walk. I'm starting to stiffen up again from sitting."

"Go with her," Etta commanded, waving her hand at Kjartan.

"No, really..." Annie protested.

Kjartan swiped a napkin across his mouth. "I'll walk you out."

He did more than that, escorting her all the way back to the house. Annie was grateful Kjartan was a man of few words. Silence suited her mood.

When they reached the house, he said, "Let me show you where the washer is." He led her to the downstairs utility room and briefly explained how to operate his machine.

There was nothing particularly intimate about the lecture, but Annie could barely listen to him for fear of falling under his spell. No matter how insistent her head, her body still felt the pull of unwanted attraction. She wanted to reach for him, kiss him, lead him upstairs. Wanted to take back yesterday afternoon so she could have spent the night in his arms. Wanted to tell him she was sorry, wanted him to say it, too, so they could get on with the business of their brief, intense romance.

"Okay?"

Annie startled back to earth. "What?"

"Do you understand?"

"Oh, yes. Sure. It looks easy. Soap here, push this button."

Kjartan nodded, that same look in his eyes as before. Was he laughing at her? Testing her? Did he know what effect being this close to him had on her?

"Annie..."

She would not give in to this weakness. Annie steeled her gaze. "Yes?"

Kjartan glanced down, reached for her fingers. "Annie, I'm so sorry. Please don't be angry."

The sigh bubbled up from the chambers of her heart, out through her tight lips. "It doesn't matter."

His hand was warm. She craved the familiar roughness of his fingers. She craved more than that—a kiss, an embrace, some evidence that she was still having this dream.

He squeezed her hand. "I'll see you tonight. Five-thirty."

"Five-thirty."

He left her standing in the hall, her throat still constricted with the words she had meant to say.

13

He looked better than she had ever seen him.

Freshly showered and shaven, his face tight from the razor. He wore pleated black wool pants and a gray wool sweater that perfectly offset his blondish-brown hair and soft brown eyes. His hair was still slightly damp, and the wind had tousled it just the way Annie liked. She had to resist running her fingers through it. He looked comfortable—rested, relaxed. It took more will than she thought she had not to pull him into the cottage and replay the scene from a few nights before.

"You look great." Annie tore her eyes away. She gestured toward her own outfit. "But are they going to let me in?" She wore jeans—clean, at least—and the pale purple sweater she had packed at the last moment just in case she needed something more formal than fleece.

"You could go in a bathrobe," Kjartan answered. "You're beautiful."

Forget dinner and kiss me, Annie prayed.

Kjartan held the door. "Are you ready?"

The restaurant was half an hour away, in the opposite direction of town. It sat alone just off the road, a yellow steel-sided building with a red steel roof.

The hostess was a girl of no more than twelve. She had long white-blond hair gathered into a braid. She greeted Kjartan gaily and called something toward the kitchen. A tall man with curly brown hair emerged, wiping his hands on his apron. He shook Kjartan's hand, then Annie's.

"This is my friend Magnús," Kjartan said. "He and his wife own this restaurant."

The two men spoke briefly in Icelandic while Annie stood politely silent. She recognized only one word: Arizona. Magnús nodded and smiled with approval at Annie.

He led them to a table by the window, with a view of the black volcanic mountain across the road.

"What a lovely place this is," Annie said.

Magnús smiled. "*Takk.*" He excused himself and returned to the kitchen.

Diners crowded the small room. Annie could hear every conversation around her, even though she couldn't understand a word.

"Is everyone here Icelandic?"

Kjartan scanned the room. "*Já.*"

"Do you know all of them?"

"*Já.*"

"Then that would explain why they're all looking at us."

Kjartan leaned forward. "One thing to remember: Even though you can't understand them, they can all understand you." He lowered his voice to a barely audible whisper. "If you need to say anything interesting, you should tell me like this."

Annie felt her resistance melting. What was the point in going out with him and not having a good time? She leaned in close. "Like this?"

"Yes. So if you want to say, 'Kjartan, I missed you last night...'"

Annie gulped. She whispered as softly as she could, "Kjartan, I missed you last night."

"I missed you, too. So much."

Annie felt warmth spread across her cheeks. She whispered, "I'm sorry."

"I am, too."

The waitress arrived. Annie snapped upright. Kjartan didn't hide his amusement. Slowly he leaned back in his chair.

The waitress greeted Kjartan warmly and rattled off a what

seemed to be a hundred words of Icelandic, all of them melodic, all incomprehensible to Annie.

Kjartan switched to English, which Annie took as her cue to pay attention.

"Annie, this is Halla, Magnús' wife. She teaches at the school. Annie is a teacher, too."

The woman offered her hand.

"Do I know you?" Annie asked.

"From the school this morning."

"Oh, right—in the kitchen." This close, the woman's hair seemed almost white—the same white-blond as the young hostess. No doubt they were mother and daughter.

"So you work at the school and here?"

"I work in the kitchen at the school sometimes when there are groups staying there. Our restaurant is busiest in the summer, so I work here, too. In the winter, not so much."

"What do you teach?"

The woman grabbed one of the few empty chairs in the room and set it next to Annie. "I teach the youngest ones—five to seven or eight, depending on how many we have each year. What age do you teach?"

"High school. Mostly fourteen-year-olds. I teach English."

"Oh, English! We need an English teacher—did Kjartan tell you?" Halla stole a look at him.

"No, someone else did." Annie hurried to head off the question she suspected would follow. While she was already reconsidering her plan to leave on Friday with Etta and Wilhelm, that only delayed her departure to the following week. "Good luck," she said. "I hope you find someone soon."

Halla did not give up so easily. "If you like, I can show you around the school next time I see you."

"No, that's okay—"

"Really, I'd like to. You can tell me how it compares to U.S."

"Oh...sure." Annie had no intention of taking the tour, but she wanted the conversation to end.

Satisfied, the woman stood and replaced the chair. "What would you like to eat tonight?"

Annie relaxed. "I'll let the two of you choose. Surprise me."

Kjartan and Halla conversed in their private tongue. At one point Halla laughed and nodded.

Annie was suspicious. When they were alone again, she asked Kjartan if he ordered a platter of shark's meat.

"*Rotten* shark meat," he corrected. "Yes. And also ram's testicles."

"Oh, thank goodness—I'm starving."

When the wine arrived, Kjartan filled their glasses and raised his in a toast. "*Skál.*"

"Scowl," Annie answered, mimicking the sound. She sipped the dark, rich merlot.

Kjartan reached across the table and took her hand in his. Annie felt twenty pairs of eyes turn their way. She nearly pulled away, but Kjartan squeezed her hand and said, "Don't. It's okay."

And suddenly it was okay. The truth was, she wanted him to hold her hand. She wanted him to show affection, to treat her tenderly, to look at her the way he was. She was here for another week and a half, she decided, and she might as well enjoy everything Kjartan and Iceland had to offer.

She rested her thumb on top of his. "Okay."

Annie sipped her wine. She rarely drank at home, but tonight was a night for letting go of some of her control. She let Kjartan stroke her fingers while they talked about the horses and putting up hay and about Sophie and Guy's departure.

The food—a tender white fish lightly fried, sautéed spinach, the ubiquitous tiny white potatoes—was excellent. The wine—all two and a half glasses of it—was very fine as well.

In some ways it was like a first date, except that Annie was not nervous. She knew this man better, she supposed, than she had known Mark. Despite all their misunderstandings, the truth was she trusted Kjartan in a way she never had Mark. Or any other man, for that matter.

"Who is your family?" he asked, spearing one of her potatoes with his fork.

"Two brothers, James and Todd. We had a younger brother—Brian—but he died when he was eight."

"Sorry."

"Yeah, it was pretty awful. Brian was my baby, you know? But both my mother and he had heart problems. My mother was doing okay until a few years ago. She died last year."

Kjartan nodded thoughtfully. "My brother and I lost both our parents young. Do you still have a father?"

"Not really. He left not long after Brian died—said he didn't want to wait around for the rest of us to die." Annie scoffed and shook her head. "Not a very brave man. He remarried eventually and had some more kids."

"Do you ever see him?"

"Nope. I've never met his kids, either. It's like we all pretend his first marriage never happened." The merlot was loosening her tongue. It felt good to talk to him about her life.

"You remember what you said about Marta?" she ventured.

Had he stiffened at that? Annie couldn't tell.

She continued, "About how you thought she was right to leave if she couldn't be happy?"

Kjartan nodded warily.

"I'm not sure I agree with that." Annie took another sip. "I think outright misery is bad, but I'm not so sure a little misery should stop someone from sticking around. Do you know what I mean? I think if you sign up for marriage, the other person should be able to count on you when things are hard."

She waited for any comment Kjartan might have. None.

"When Brian died it was hard on all of us—not just my father. But we lived through it, you know? Nobody tried to run away." Annie tore off a piece of bread and swiped it across her plate. She bit off a chunk and shrugged. "That's just what I think. So you have a brother?"

Kjartan paused before answering. Annie wondered what he thought of her ramblings. "Thorsten. He lives in Isafjordur."

"How old is he?"

Kjartan squinted as he calculated. "Thirty-two? Thirty-three?"

"Do you ever see him?"

"*Já*. Holidays—Christmas, sometimes Easter. Not so much in the summer because it's a busy time. Do you see your brothers?"

"We try to get together a few times a year. James lives in Denver and Todd lives in Phoenix. My cousin Shannon and her brothers go backpacking every year, and my brothers and I usually go along. It's a nice time for us all to see each other."

They talked more about their backgrounds—education, jobs, families—but gradually Annie felt the fog of merlot closing in. Normally one glass was enough to make her sleepy. Two and a half made her tongue slow, her eyelids droop.

"Would you like me to take you home?"

Home. It sounded so nice. A home she might share with him tonight, if he asked her. "Yes, please."

Kjartan bade the chef and his wife goodbye and led Annie to the van.

He held her hand so softly, so sweetly, Annie thought she might have to cry. Why had she wasted a night being angry with him? Why had she wasted a single hour?

Looking at the bright summer sky, she had no idea what time it was. Her watch was back in the cottage. What difference did it make? Kjartan had said it himself: In Iceland, forget about time. She would sleep when she was sleepy, awaken when she was rested. What mattered was whether she slept alone or with Kjartan. And that mattered very much.

Inside the privacy of the van, Annie reached for Kjartan's hand and pulled him to her. She kissed him tentatively, testing her own wine-muddled reaction to the contact. She felt dizzy, and decided she liked it that way. She cupped her hands around Kjartan's face and kissed him with as much passion as she could bear. He ran his hands along her sides, flirting with the edges of her breasts.

Annie ached to feel him closer. "I missed you so much last night."

"Sleep with me tonight."

Annie nodded and kissed him again. "Maybe tonight we should sleep with fewer clothes."

"I think that is a terrible idea," Kjartan answered. He sat back against the seat to catch his breath. "I have to drive now. Please keep your distance."

Annie laughed. "Do you know how good you look tonight?" She reached over and tucked a tuft of hair behind his ear. "I can barely stand looking at you. Do you know how bad I want to—"

Kjartan captured her hand and kissed it. Then he planted it firmly on her lap. "No more. I have to drive. Wait until we're home."

The wine continued its course through her system, making Annie doze on the ride back. Kjartan awakened her with a kiss. Annie pulled him to her and deepened the kiss, pulling away only when she needed air.

"Annie, come upstairs."

As they climbed the stairs together, she felt such a deep longing to be with him, she was afraid of what she might say. It was more than just her physical ache to make love to him that night. What she felt was a deep, raw need to discover every part of him, to hold him safe within her heart, to love him as much as they both deserved and to let that love grow at its own perfect pace.

What she did not want was a deadline. She didn't want to arrive at next Saturday when she would climb up a different set of stairs, into a cramped airplane, out of his life.

When they were safe behind a locked door, Annie poured out her love through her eyes. "I don't want to leave you," she said, regretting it immediately. The wine had made her too free. She needed to protect them both.

"Then don't," he said. He drew her close and kissed her. "Stay with me as long as you want."

"I will," she answered, knowing eleven days was only a fraction of the time she needed.

"Papa! Kjartan is here with a lady!" the young hostess had announced. Instantly every eye in the restaurant was on them.

The reactions of his friends Magnús and Halla, and those of the diners, confirmed for Kjartan just how solitary he had become.

Why had he brought her there? Was it to show her off, like a new foal? Or was it to give her a taste of life outside the farm? Maybe he wanted her to know that she would not be confined to eating at the school and in his cramped, tourist-laden kitchen.

Or maybe, he thought more charitably, it was just to enjoy

her company in a pleasant setting and to discover more about this woman who had captured his interest.

She was like him in more ways than he would have guessed. She had a strong sense of duty that took priority over comfort and pleasure. She did not say it this way, but he understood: She had sacrificed much for her mother, and did not regret any of it.

She told him she had been accepted by universities all over the country, but had chosen to stay in Tucson. She had job opportunities—Colorado, Utah, California—but she accepted a position in town. While her brothers married and moved away, Annie stayed in place to do what she could for her mother, whether it was shopping for her or taking her to the doctors or sitting with her in the evenings watching movies.

In the last three months of her mother's life, Annie had taken a leave of absence from the school and moved in with her mother. She provided round-the-clock care, even though her brothers had offered to help Annie pay for a nurse. Annie knew her mother's peculiarities about being touched and being seen. She didn't want to distress her mother further.

Annie had told him all this without a hint of martyrdom, just as if she had been describing her course of study at the university. To his view, she saw her duty and she acted. He respected her for that.

Sitting at the table holding Annie's hand in full view of many of his neighbors, Kjartan had felt content. He didn't wish to prove anything to any of them, he wanted to prove it to himself: If he wanted to, he could love again. He could crawl out of his cave. There was warmth and satisfaction out here in the light.

Annie was asleep almost as soon as she hit the bed. Kjartan covered her with the blanket then lay down beside her.

She slept with her hands under her face, just as she had in the van the morning she arrived. Kjartan played with the ends of her silky hair. She was so lovely, so kind. The more he learned about her, the more convinced he was of that. He kissed her cheek softly and wrapped his arms around her.

"Annie," he whispered, "I love you."

The moment he said it he knew it was true. Impossible, but true.

She was lively and beautiful and complicated. He felt a deep need for her that he knew he would have to deny a few nights more. Sleeping with her chastely had done more to convince him of his feelings than if they had made love all night. As incredible as it was, he knew she was the woman of his life. Now the question was what he could do about it.

She could have died the day before. That fact had left its mark on him. While outwardly he mastered his emotions and arranged for the group to go on, inside he was seriously shaken by how narrowly she had escaped being crushed by the horse.

It left with him with two conflicting thoughts: First, that she was not fit for life on his farm, with its constant dangers from machinery, animals, and weather. Or rather, he could not afford to worry about her, which he suspected he would all the time. He needed a partner he could trust to stand up to inevitable hardship. It was why he had put up with Petra for so long. For all of her faults, she was an excellent horsewoman and a hard worker. Annie didn't have the skills necessary to live in comfort there.

The second thought was this: I don't want to live without her.

While his heart thudded in his chest and his hands methodically checked her for injuries, his mind told him, *Don't let her go. Ask her to stay.* He didn't want to lose a day with her. He didn't want to let her go.

When he awoke that morning, his head aching from too little sleep and too much contemplation, he thought he knew what he should do. He would start over, court her, win her. He would introduce her to Halla and plant the seed about Annie staying on, working there, living there.

She mumbled something and snuggled closer to him. Kjartan rested his chin on her head. He listened to the rhythm of her breathing.

"Annie, I love you," hoping she would wake up and catch him saying it.

But what about the practicalities? his analytical mind pestered. This woman has a life—a full life somewhere, with a job, and friends, and family. She's here for only a short time—shorter now with each hour. This isn't her life—never will be. To pretend otherwise is to invite a shattered heart.

His sleep was fitful. Each time he awoke and found her still wrapped within his arms, he prodded himself to say something.

Don't let her go. Ask her to stay...

Even if she agreed, how could they ever make it work? Annie had lived her whole life in a place bathed in sunlight. What chance did Kjartan have of keeping her happy through even one dark season? What chance did he have, separating her from everything that was familiar, from everyone she loved? Why put them both through that, when he already knew the likely outcome?

Kjartan had already watched one wife grow more depressed with each year—he couldn't bear to see it in Annie. Marta was a native Icelander, but even she couldn't tolerate the winter's murky light and harsh, intemperate weather. Some Icelanders reveled in winter, seeing it as the natural balance to summer's frenzy. Others, like Marta, saw it as an annual sentence of death.

No matter how optimistic he wanted to be, Kjartan was still a practical man. Wishing for something had never made it happen.

Annie was his for now—wasn't that enough? Wasn't that more than he had before?

Too soon she would remember her other life, when she awakened from this dream they had spun together. Until then, he would love her as much as he could—as much as she would let him.

Don't let her go. Ask her to stay...

Impossible. Like asking the sun not to set.

14

Annie pretended to wander. No one was watching, so she knew she wasn't pretending for anyone's sake but her own. She would just see, she thought. No harm in looking.

She had awakened early to find Kjartan already gone. She still wore her jeans and sweater from the night before. Kjartan hadn't undressed her. What a gentleman, Annie thought. She smiled to herself. What a chicken.

Just one more day. One more day of this platonic sleeping. One more day and then they would see.

Back in her cottage she showered and shaved. She dressed in jeans and her long underwear top, then trudged toward the school for a cup of coffee that could not be strong enough.

The cafeteria was empty. Petra must have risen early, too, because the food table was set up and, Annie was grateful to find, the coffee pot was full. She poured a cup of *kaffi* and added a splash of *mjólk*.

She studied the carton for a moment. She knew some Icelandic words by sight now: *mjólk* for milk, the misleading name *appelsínusafi* for orange juice, *morgunkorn* for cereal. *Smjör* meant butter. *Fiskur* was fish. Her mind recognized the letters now through repetition, but she couldn't really read them. She could imagine the frustration of illiteracy: to know a stop sign said "stop"—to know that other letters in certain sequences meant other things—but not be able to read the words.

She loved to hear Kjartan speak Icelandic. She loved the sound of it—the purr of the r's, the soft "th" sound for the "d" in words like *Isafjordur*, where Kjartan's brother lived—but she wasn't secure enough in her own powers of mimicry to pronounce the words correctly. So far the only word she used with regularity was *takk* for thank you. That one was easy.

She decided then she would make more of an effort to learn Icelandic. She wanted to understand the things Kjartan said. Rather than tune out when those around her spoke Icelandic, she would have to pay close attention. She had heard that some immigrants to America learned English by watching soap operas. For the next week or so, she would immerse herself in conversational Icelandic and see if she could pick up something besides "milk" and "thank you."

Kaffi in hand, she wandered out of the cafeteria toward the wing of the school which held the classrooms. She padded softly in her socks across the linoleum, pretending not to care about her destination.

She opened the door to one of the classrooms. Small—as small as an elementary school room—with tables instead of desks, and full-size chairs instead of the bite-size ones American children were given. Eight chairs per table, just as in the cafeteria. Only three tables, so twenty-four students at most.

She looked out the windows toward the pastures behind the school. Part of Kjartan's herd ran there. A river snaked through the grass. Annie had seen Wilhelm fishing there many times.

What would a teacher's life be like there? Annie took a moment to test whether she really, sincerely wanted to play this game. *What if...what if you stayed? What would your life look like? What would you be?*

She granted herself two minutes. Two minutes to fantasize, then no more.

Go...

She would wake up next to Kjartan every morning.

No, she thought, he would wake up before her and leave quietly, the way he had that morning.

She would bundle up in every piece of clothing she had—

where would she get clothes? What did people wear during the winter in Iceland?—*You're using up your two minutes...*

...and she would walk to the school. Maybe she would eat breakfast there with the children.

The children. What might they be like? She knew most of them didn't learn English until they were eleven, so there would be pantomime and friendly smiles from some of them, words she could recognize from others.

She would have to learn the language. She could, couldn't she? It had been a long time since she'd studied French, but hadn't that been easy for her to learn? Did she have a facility with language, or was she making that up?

Time's almost up...

Teach all day—teach whatever they needed her to teach— English, maybe history—wouldn't that be fascinating to learn? Would she teach from the sagas?

Walk home. Cook dinner. In the winter there would be no night rides to keep Kjartan from her. He would be hers all night, to have and to hold...

Bzzz! Wake up.

Stop it, Annie told herself. Giving in to the fantasy would only make it worse. She was leaving next week. No amount of pretending could change that.

Annie closed the door.

She returned to the cafeteria where a few early risers sat sipping coffee and smoking. She refilled her cup and chose an empty table. Soon Etta and Wilhelm arrived.

"Last day," Wilhelm mourned.

"What happened?" Etta asked. It took a moment for Annie to realize she was asking about the date.

"I had the fish," Annie answered mischievously.

Etta rolled her eyes. "Tell me what happened."

Kjartan loomed large in the doorway. She was wrong: He didn't look best with a gray sweater and a clean-shaven face. He looked best like this: hair askew from a night sleeping beside her, blond stubble, eyes tired but gazing at her softly, the hint of a smile intended only for her. Shyly, Annie returned the smile.

When had anyone ever looked at her that way, as if she were a great treasure to admire? When had she ever felt this way—so giddy, so alive, so...loved? Wasn't that what she saw in his sleepy, gentle gaze? Wasn't that what she had heard him whisper in her dream last night?

How was she going to leave him behind? How could this possibly end?

Kjartan came to her and kissed her on the cheek. He greeted his other guests, then sat beside Annie and reached for her hand. Etta would not stop smiling. Annie let her have her way.

"I have a ride to do tonight," Kjartan said. "Someone just called. Six people. Will you come with me?"

Annie doused the flicker of fear in her chest. "Yes—if you'll show me what to do the next time my horse decides to run away with me."

"There are a lot of things I can tell you now that you have a little experience. Do you want to go try after breakfast?"

"You don't have anything else to do?"

"I always have things to do. But I'd rather help you."

Etta beamed. She leaned toward Wilhelm and mumbled something in German. From the look on Kjartan's face, Annie suspected he both overheard and understood the remark.

Kjartan squeezed Annie's hand. "I'll eat, then we'll go practice, okay?"

While he assembled his breakfast, Etta interrogated Annie.

"Did he say anything last night?"

"Yes."

"What?"

"The horses will be getting their winter coats soon. One of the mares is limping—"

Etta didn't hide her irritation. "You know what I'm asking. Did he tell you he loves you?"

"No!" Annie leaned forward, hoping to encourage Etta to lower her voice.

"He does, you know. I can see it."

"Is that what you said to Wilhelm a minute ago, in front of Kjartan?"

"Yes," Wilhelm verified.

"I wanted Kjartan to hear," Etta announced. "Did you see his face? He didn't deny it, did he?"

"Etta, you need to stop this. You're putting too much pressure—"

"I leave the day after tomorrow. An old woman does not have time to be discreet."

"You are not an old woman, and there's always time to be discreet. Please, just stop this now. You're making both of us nervous."

Kjartan returned to the table.

"I don't make you nervous, do I?" Etta asked. Annie shot her a glare, which Etta promptly ignored. "Everyone here knows what is happening, don't we?"

Kjartan raised an eyebrow, but said nothing. He smeared butter on his toast.

Etta looked at her husband, at Annie, back at Kjartan. "Well? Do I have to ask all the questions?"

Kjartan layered cheese and jam on his toast and took a bite. He answered softly, "What do you want to know?"

He didn't seem the slightest bit concerned what Etta might say next. Why was he playing along? Annie wondered. Couldn't he see where this was going?

"Etta," Annie tried, "I don't think—"

Etta waved her hand dismissively. "I want to know do you love this woman or don't you?"

Kjartan took another bite of toast. He chewed a few times. His mouth full, he answered, "*Já.*"

There it was again, the "yes" that sounded like "no." Before Annie's heart could register any pain, Kjartan swallowed and translated for her. "Yes. I do."

Annie barely had time to absorb the declaration before Etta turned on her. "And do you?"

"What?" Annie's heart thundered in her chest.

"Do you love him?"

"Etta, stop it—this isn't funny."

Etta turned to the others for support. "Am I making a joke? I am very serious. Do you love Kjartan?"

Annie stood, the blood pounding in her ears. This was not

how she imagined it at all. She felt like a display mannequin, like an actress playing a part. Kjartan continued eating, no hint of emotion on his face. Was this a joke to him, too? Was the whole thing so easy for him?

"You know, Etta, some things are personal, all right?" Annie left the table abruptly, ignoring Etta's call to return.

Annie's eyes burned. She pulled on her boots as quickly as she could, mindful that Kjartan was walking toward her. She didn't wait. She stepped into the cold, bright morning and hiked toward the farm.

Kjartan took up his place beside her. From the corner of her eye she saw him looking at her.

He waited until they were halfway down the road. "Are you okay?"

She wasn't sure she knew herself. She shook her head and said nothing.

Kjartan walked silently beside her. Annie longed to reach for his hand, but couldn't allow herself do it. An incredible urge for self-preservation had taken hold, and she had to trust that instinct.

Annie was just about to turn onto the footpath leading to her cottage when Kjartan said, "Would you come upstairs for a moment?"

Annie was both grateful and reluctant. "Why?"

"I want to talk to you."

He closed the bedroom door behind them and perched on the end of the bed. Annie sat near him on the other bed. Kjartan held out his arm for her. With a sigh, Annie surrendered. She wanted to be close. She scooted across the divide and leaned her head against his shoulder. He wrapped his arm around her.

He didn't ask her anything. Just waited.

"Every day," she began, "is one day less."

"I know."

"Everyone acts like they know exactly what's going to happen with us, but I have to tell you, I don't know." She tilted her head to look at him. "I'm not asking you to tell me, because I don't think you know, either."

"No, I don't."

She rested against him once more. "I just feel like hiding out right now. I'm sick of people watching us and nudging each other and asking so many questions..."

Kjartan leaned back on the bed, bringing Annie with him. He gathered her in closer so that her cheek rested on his heart.

"What do you think about?" he asked her.

"What do you mean?" she stalled, knowing exactly what he meant.

"Do you ever think about next week?"

Annie's stomach tightened. "I'm trying not to."

"Don't you think we should?"

"No."

Kjartan was silent for a time. Annie settled more deeply into their embrace. It was nice there, just the two of them, nothing and no one to interfere.

"I have to leave on Friday," Kjartan said.

"What? Why?"

"It's just for three days. Some doctors from Reykjavik want to go on a longer tour."

"Oh." Annie's heart felt leaden. "Okay."

She started to pull away, but Kjartan held her fast. "Come with me."

"What's the point?" Annie murmured into his chest.

"The point is I love you, and I want to spend as much time with you as I can."

Tears burned her eyes. Somehow hearing him say it again made her feel worse.

"I have to leave next week," she choked.

"I know."

She lifted her head to look at him. There it was again, that soft gleam in his eyes, that look of tenderness that threatened to melt her every objection.

"Kjartan, I can't—"

He quieted her with a kiss. She gave in to it, wanting impulse to overcome her common sense.

What had she started to say? "I can't because—" Because I'm afraid, she thought, of falling too deeply into this fantasy. Because I'm afraid of getting too comfortable here. Because I'm afraid of how natural it feels to be in your home, in your bed, in your arms. I can break my own heart here, with no help from you. I can do it alone just by wanting this too much.

"It's just a crush," Annie murmured. "You don't even know me."

He kissed her eyes, her cheeks. "Will you come with me Friday?"

She nodded and offered her lips again.

But Kjartan was suddenly all business. "Let's go down to the stable. I want to show you to ride."

15

She had meant to keep it a secret until after the ride. But seeing him standing in the rain in his long duster and worn hat, hearing him bark orders to Petra and politely answer the multitude of questions from his customers, and catching the intimate glance he threw her way in the midst of all his activity, Annie knew she had to tell him.

As Kjartan tied the leather pouch filled with sandwiches onto the back of his saddle, Annie stepped close and murmured, "It's tonight." Then she turned and started to walk away.

He caught her by the hood of her raincoat, and discreetly pulled her back. "Tonight, what?"

She smiled sleepily, with that same lethargy that seemed to overtake her whenever the attraction felt too great. "You know what."

They didn't speak of it again. Kjartan herded the customers into the van, drove them to the same remote pasture where Annie had begun her first ride, herded the horses, helped the riders with their selections. He paired Annie with a tan mare she thought she might have ridden before, but she didn't ask him about it. She didn't want to talk. Kjartan, too, kept his words to himself. Annie imagined his mind was as occupied as hers.

This time she knew the way. She pulled the horse into line behind Petra and two other riders, and immediately settled into the *tölt*.

Kjartan had practiced with her for over an hour that morning in the small pasture beside his stable. First he showed her how to halt a runaway horse by pulling the reins to one side and diverting the horse from its line. He showed her how to ride more comfortably by tucking her hips and relaxing her shoulders and spine. He corrected her leg position and the way she held her reins. She practiced pulling her boots out of the stirrups then slipping them back in again while the horse was still moving.

Kjartan explained the psychology of the horse as a prey animal, as a herd animal, and told her how to reassure a skittish mount by maintaining firm control. Most of all, he said, she should retain her own composure no matter what happened—that alone would reduce whatever risks she might face.

A light rain sputtered down. Annie's mare hurried up the hillside toward the vast overhang of cliffs. Annie felt that same urgency. She wanted the ride to be over, wanted to be home again, alone with Kjartan. As he rode past her he brushed the back of his hand across her thigh. He briefly consulted with Petra, then rode back toward his place in the rear. As he passed her he flashed Annie a sly smile and said, "Tonight we take the short way."

At the fork in the trails, Petra led the group across the lowland route. It was the same route Kjartan had scolded her for taking the night of Annie's first ride. Annie smiled in private appreciation. The sooner the better, my love.

She hadn't told him back.

All day long she had pushed the thought away, but here it was again.

He told her he loved her and she had just accepted it without comment.

Why hadn't she said it back?

Because, Annie reasoned, she had never said it—not to a man, not to her mother, not to her brothers, not to anyone.

She could write it. E-mails and letters were no problem. Shannon got to see the words all the time, but so far she had never heard Annie say them.

There was something private—almost shameful—about

saying it out loud, as if Annie were called upon to undress in public. She had never heard her mother say it once—not casually, not accidentally, not even as she lay dying. Annie knew her mother loved her, of course, but the message had always been clear: We don't say it. That's personal. That's giving too much away.

Luckily none of her relationships with men had ever gotten that far. Mark had hung around the longest, but since he never said it, she never had to confront the issue. She was grateful for that, since the truth was she never felt that way toward him. She liked him, was attracted to him, respected him, but did not love.

But she did love Kjartan. She knew it days before when they sat holding hands in front of the store. It was more than a crush, more than electric attraction. She felt a quiet connection to him that didn't rest on what they said to each other or how they touched or even how lovingly he treated her.

She felt, as Sophie had once told her, that she was compelled to come to Iceland. That everything in her life had led her to this place, this time, this man.

That she and Kjartan were born to love each other.

So why didn't she tell him?

When they reached the first beach, Kjartan rode up beside her. "How do you feel? All right?"

"Yes. Very well. This mare is perfect for me."

The other riders galloped ahead, but Annie held back. Even though she felt more comfortable than ever on the horse, she still felt the limitations of her fear. Kjartan matched her speed and stayed by her side. The two *tölted* across the sand.

He changed their pace so gradually, Annie didn't notice at first. But midway across the long stretch of beach, she couldn't deny it any longer: the horses were galloping. She could have stopped it—could have called to Kjartan to slow down—but she didn't. She wanted this. She wanted to feel the speed of the horse's legs pounding against the sand, feel the cold wet wind blowing in from the sea. She wanted to feel herself take a risk—like skinny dipping, like kissing Kjartan that first time. She wanted to feel herself let go.

She knew Kjartan couldn't protect her from everything, but

she felt safe with him riding at her side. He must have thought she was ready for this, Annie reasoned, and his confidence fed hers. She let herself enjoy it. She deliberately fought off fear. As they raced along the edge of the sea, she tried to see herself as she was, there in that moment, this version of herself that she had never known existed.

This—this picture of the two of them riding side by side on a black sand beach under a sun that refused to set—wasn't this as different as her life had ever been? Who was this blond man in the wide leather hat, this man who would hold her that night and perhaps every night if she would let him? And who was the woman at his side, with the pageboy hair and the clothes not quite right and the easy, joyous smile as she galloped into the wind? Who could imagine such people? Who could imagine such a life?

At the end of the beach Annie tugged back the reins. To her relief the horse slowed, then stopped. Annie was out of breath. Her head felt light. A wave of joy swept over her, so consuming she thought it might overflow and flood her out of her own skin.

Kjartan pulled up along side her. "Annie, that was perfect."

She nudged her horse closer and leaned out of the saddle. She wrapped her arms around Kjartan's neck and kissed him so hard she thought their lips would bleed.

"Thank you." Her smile was so wide she could feel new muscles in her face. She kissed him again, tasting the cold, wet salt on their lips.

"Keep going. I want to take you home." Kjartan clicked his horse back into motion. Annie followed, her heart warm with pleasure.

When they reached the lava field, the horses slowed to pick their way among the rocks. Annie swayed in the saddle, hips tucked in the way Kjartan had showed her, the rest of her body relaxed. Kjartan was in front of her now, Petra at the back. Once more Annie reveled in the sight of the tall blond rider atop his sturdy blond horse, as they rode across the field of black lava and bright green moss. The sky was concrete gray, the light a muted gold. She wanted to remember those colors. She wished she had a camera or that she could paint, so she could always remember how Kjartan looked at that moment.

Midway through the field Kjartan let the horses graze. He invited the riders on a tour of the lava cave. Annie followed at the rear.

When they had seen enough, the riders climbed back into the light. Annie and Kjartan hung back.

He pulled her deeper into the utter darkness of the cave and pressed his hungry mouth to hers.

"You shouldn't have told me," he said. "I can't think." He slipped his cold hand beneath her shirt. She jerked away involuntarily. "Sorry," he said.

Annie laid her hand over his. "No, leave it there."

Kjartan groaned. "We have to go."

"Let Petra take them. We'll stay here." She pressed against him, aching to be rid of their clothes. She slipped her hand beneath his duster and felt him respond. He pressed his thigh between hers in seductive retaliation.

"We have to go." Kjartan gripped her arms and held her off. He avoided her lips and kissed her chastely on the cheek. "I can't ride like this. Go on. I'll be there in a minute."

She couldn't resist trailing her finger across him one last time.

"Uch, Annie." He caught her hand. "I have to drive."

The last stretch home over the flat spongy ground felt light and easy. Annie brought her horse into the *tölt* and closed her eyes, enjoying the gentle sway of her hips. The movement aroused her—not because straddling a horse felt especially provocative, but because she imagined the rhythm, the motion, the rise and sway of her hips against her lover.

In the stable she attended to the mare methodically. She didn't pause as she had other times to watch the horses roll in the dust, so giddy to be free of their saddles. She put away her gear and left without looking at Kjartan. Not looking at him filled her with a wicked pleasure. They both knew. They didn't have to say anything.

She stood in the hot shower, her mind deliberately blank. She didn't want to think about him. She wanted to surprise herself—

to give herself completely to the sensation of lovemaking. She didn't want her fantasies of him to dilute the thrill of reality. She would come to him open, unafraid, without rules or expectations.

She dressed simply, no underclothes, just pants, shirt, boots.

Into the house. Boots off. Quietly up the stairs. She could hear the shower running. She closed the door and locked it, then leaned against it, waiting.

He came out of the bathroom naked. He didn't hesitate. He strode toward her and swept her into his arms.

His hands grazed her breasts through her shirt. She reached down to pull the shirt over her head, but he stopped her.

"Go slow. We have all night."

She touched him lightly, trickling her fingers down his belly, lower.

"Annie..." His mouth covered hers and drove the heat from her head to her toes.

They fell onto the bed. He freed her of her shirt, then her pants and then they were skin to skin, nothing to stop them, no barriers but what their minds might invent.

No hurry. The sky was still light. They had all night for this pleasure. No rush at all.

When the moment seemed upon them, Annie murmured, "*Smokkar.*"

Kjartan laughed. "You're learning." He reached for the bedside table and pulled open the drawer. He tore off one from a string of condoms.

"When did you get those?"

"When you locked my keys in the van."

"I didn't do that! It was Etta."

"Shhhh." His tongue teased her breast, driving any further argument from her lips. He pulled her arms above her head and licked lightly along the groove of her armpit.

"Why do you do that?" she gasped. It was a tactic so intimate, so strange, so arousing.

"I like how smooth you are here. And here...and here..."

She pulled the pillow over her face to muffle her cries.

When the time was right he reached for the condom and

deftly slipped it on. Then he entered her gently, slowly, no break in the rhythm of their sighs and moans.

For the first time with a man, she felt no fear. She surrendered everything to him, knowing he would treasure what she was, what she gave. She loved without hesitation, without boundaries. When she drew him into her she abandoned what little resistance she had left. This was what she wanted. This was what she had. He gave her as much as she had ever imagined was possible. He made love to her as if he knew every fear, every lie, every hurt that had ever darkened her heart. He stripped them away and revealed what was fine and perfect and whole, and he made her believe she could live like this, could love this much and not have to turn away from it. He carried her with him to the brink of the ledge and then pulled her down with him and she was falling and she was not afraid. She wanted all that he was and all that he loved in her, and she wanted it for the rest of her life, not just the rest of this night.

When he cried out for her, gripped her shoulders, pulled his mouth to hers, she didn't have to think about what to do. Her body moved naturally, her hips rocking slowly, while she savored the sighs that told her he couldn't last much longer.

He tensed, moaned, drove hard to the release. Annie held her breath, waited for his body to relax. This was as much as she had ever known. She lowered her lips to his, satisfied as long as he was satisfied.

But Kjartan had other ideas. He rolled her onto her back. He tested pressure, rhythm, location. When she moaned and arched her back, he stayed there. It was too much, too deep, too rich. Annie tried to pull his hand away.

"No," he whispered, "let me."

Now she was afraid. He was turning her inside out. But she trusted him, believed him, wanted him to try.

And then the tears came. Hot on her face with the coming heat between her thighs. She reached back for the pillow to cover her face. Kjartan gripped her wrist. "No, let me see you." He kissed her and moved her and carried her high up the cliff then pushed her over the edge and she was there, not falling, but safe. Safe and protected and soaring.

She sobbed—deep, wrenching cries that shook her body and soaked her cheeks. Kjartan licked at the tears, then brushed his salty tongue against her lips.

She rolled onto her side and cried, not knowing when it would stop or why it had come. She was happy, wasn't she? She had never been happier. But he had torn away the last of her armor, and now she lay naked and exposed and in love.

Tears gave way to exhaustion. She had nothing left to give.

Kjartan cradled her from behind. He wrapped his hand in hers and folded it into her heart. He kissed the back of her head.

Don't say anything, Annie thought. Was she telling herself or him?

"Good night," Kjartan whispered.

It sounded just right.

Annie closed her eyes and settled against him. "Good night."

The next morning, the e-mail to her principal seemed to compose itself.

16

Six hours in the saddle, but she was finally getting used to it. Kjartan rode ahead, his two alternate horses trailing behind on their leads. Annie rode in second position, the four doctors behind her. All led their extra two horses, and at stops along the way switched the saddle and head gear to a fresh horse for the next few hours. Annie preferred the first and third horse she rode that day, with their narrow backs and easy strides. The middle horse had the uncomfortable habit of falling out of the *tölt* every few miles, jarring Annie from the scenery back to the mechanics of getting the horse to do anything but trot.

She rode in silence. During breaks Kjartan spoke to her briefly, but he spent most of his time answering questions from the doctors and tending to the eighteen horses. Annie watched him with distant admiration. He moved with an unconscious grace, with an efficiency born of experience and natural skill. She couldn't imagine him living any life other than this. She tried to conjure a picture of him sitting at a desk in an office in the city, going to meetings, talking on the phone. What a slow death for a man like this. He needed the air and the sunlight and the wind, the rain streaming off his hat, his muddy boots, his chapped, dirty hands, the smell of horse and hay and sweat.

Did Annie have a secret life like that? she wondered. Was she sitting in her own version of a prison letting her life drift away when something better—something perfectly matched to her sensibilities and skills—lay out there waiting for her to wake up from her stupor?

She loved to teach—that much she knew—but she did not love to teach freshman English. She hadn't loved that for a long time. What she missed was the enthusiasm of willing students. She missed feeling that she was doing something other than filling fifty-minute units of time, five periods a day. When was the last time she felt the spark of genuine interest—from herself or from her students? She was in a rut and she knew it. She hadn't guessed how liberating it would feel to send that e-mail the day before. *"This is to inform you..."* Fancy, formal language that Shannon had suggested, all variations on the same theme: I quit.

She hadn't told Kjartan yet. Hadn't told Shannon, either. She wasn't sure why, but she wanted it to be her secret for a while.

Yes, you know why, she scolded herself. The long ride seemed to foster these internal debates. *You know why and you won't say it. Say it.*

Because...

Because then you'd have to do something about it, wouldn't you? You'd have to make some decisions.

And there was the problem: Were they really her decisions to make?

What, exactly, did she think was going to happen? Kjartan loved her, she loved him—although she still hadn't mentioned it to him yet— and life was perfect.

No, life was a fantasy. This whole thing was a fantasy. Life—real life—was the mortgage payments on her mother's house, the medical bills she would be paying for years to come, the brothers and cousin and friends scattered across the country—another country, not this country—the responsibilities that came with living an ordinary life. Yes, she had quit her job. Yes, she had taken one bold, Freydis-like action and had freed herself from one responsibility. But in the real world people had to earn an income. What was she going to do about that? In the real world people had to go home from vacation and restart their mail and water their plants and take care of all the little things that kept life chugging along.

So Kjartan loved her—did that solve her problems? She couldn't ask him to take her in and support her. She had to work. She could teach at the school, maybe, if her credentials were good here. But there was still her mother's house, her mother's bills, all the fallout from an illness that not only killed but also impoverished. Annie's mother had left her the house, so it was her responsibility now. Annie's brothers had their own families to support—Annie couldn't ask them for more. Plus, there was the house itself—what would she do with it? She couldn't sell it, not her mother's house. She might rent it, but that would mean packing away all of their things, finding someplace to store them, on and on and on...

Okay, so we'll just walk away. The greatest love of your life, but there's that mortgage to pay...

What would Freydis do?

Freydis. Freydis would gallop past him and grab him by the hair and drag him back to her lair.

Kjartan was a worthy match for any Icelandic heroine. He was stubborn and gifted and rational. His stoic manner hid a passionate nature any woman would feel grateful to have unleashed. He made love with a sensitivity and power Annie had never imagined might exist. He melted her from the inside out, mastering her needs before she even knew what they were, showing her what was possible from love and what was necessary and how much she should have been wanting all this time. No movie, no classic romance, no fantasy had prepared her for how rich a man's touch might feel, for how deeply a tender gaze might penetrate her heart. If she were writing her own saga, there was no question what the heroine would do.

She would stay. She would stay no matter what.

At the farmhouse in the little town where they boarded that night, with the horses safely stabled and the doctors merrily engaged in a combination of drinking and bragging, Annie and Kjartan stole away to their guest cabin. They shut the door quietly behind them and then faced each other in the dim light of the bedside lamp. Then without a word they undressed each other and laid themselves bare, body and soul.

It could always be like this, Annie thought. Pure love, pure pleasure, no fear and no holding back. Didn't she want that? How could she even imagine going back to the kind of life she used to lead? How could she ask her heart to close down again—to go back to being numb—after everything it had felt in these past several days?

She loved him. She knew it with the certainty of a scientist acknowledging gravity. She accepted it as a truth, with the kind of finality afforded mathematical equations and matters of spelling. There was a right answer and a wrong one. Annie loved Kjartan. Any other interpretation of what she was feeling was simply wrong. She couldn't fight it or deny it. It simply was.

Over and over as she kissed his lips, his eyes, his fingers, his heart, she thought, *I love you, I love you.* She was a character in her own romance. She could say whatever she wanted. She had nothing to fear, no reason to feel ashamed, no excuse for keeping it hidden even one more second.

But still she didn't say it.

Instead she told him with her body, her eyes, her lips. She confessed her love through caresses and moans and sighs. Kjartan answered her with his quickening breath, with his racing pulse, and with words he wasn't ashamed to say and that Annie was grateful to hear. "I love you," he told her, and she drew him more deeply inside.

Say it!

Not now...

They united in the rocketing passion of mutual pleasure, their eyes locked in love, their bodies entwined in perfect precision, their hearts beating against each other's until they had nothing left to give.

The next day was a dream. Annie ate and saddled her horse and rode for hours not knowing where she was, knowing only that she was following. She wanted to follow, wanted to give up control and let him lead her to another life. She wanted to forget everything but this: the cold air, the black lava, the neon green moss, the gray mare beneath her, and the man that she loved astride his blond horse. In the evening she ate without tasting, waiting for the moment they could rise from the table, say goodnight to the doctors and their hosts, clasp hands as they walked to the guest cottage, undress and resume their feast of love.

Such a lovely dream. Everything she ever wanted.

On the third day a persistent thought nagged at her, always tickling the edge of her mind, forcing her to stay awake instead of slipping back into the dream.

I love him, she thought.

But what will you do now?

Not yet. Let me sleep, just a little while longer...

What will you do now? Decide. This isn't a dream...

In a way, she was relieved.

Two e-mails in her inbox.

One from Shannon: *"Did you do it?"*

From Bob Messinger, principal of Desert High: *"Resignation declined."*

She stared the subject lines, wondering which message would bring her the greater pain.

Shannon, so merry, so hopeful.

Messinger, so logical.

Annie read them both. She closed out the program, left Kjartan's office, put her boots back on and took a walk down the road from the house.

She had her tonsils out when she was young—maybe five or six. She remembered being wheeled into the operating room, already feeling sleepy from the shot they'd given her. She craned her head back to look at the doctor behind her. He cupped a mask over her mouth, fiddled with some machines, and asked her if she knew how to count backwards.

100, 99, 98...

She meant to stay awake but she couldn't.

She awoke the same way, fighting hard to stay in her dream, not wanting to feel the pain in her throat, but unable to stop herself from snapping back.

She saw it in her mother's eyes, too—that will to go on despite the demands of reality. In the end she had slipped away without wanting to. Annie had stood there, waiting for her to come back the way she always had. But not this time. Reality would always conquer hope.

So here it was again. No matter what Annie had decided, no matter how wonderful the fantasy might be, real life had its own rules.

You don't quit your job. Not when someone held your position open while you tended to family matters. Not when you already pledged to sign on for the new year. Not this close to the beginning of the semester—*"I thought better of you than that."*

So this was how it was.

When Kjartan reached for her that night, she made love to him with no less fire, but already she could feel her heart pulling away, could feel the first sheets of armor reappearing.

"Annie!" Halla called out the next morning. "Ready for your tour of the school?"

Annie invented some excuse, then ducked out of the cafeteria. The last thing she needed was to hear how welcome she would be there.

She knew Kjartan could sense the change, because he retreated into a silence that matched hers. They spent the days apart, joining again at night to express with their bodies the emotions neither of them dared talk about.

With two days to go, Kjartan said, "I'd like to drive you."

That one statement told her everything. He knew she was leaving. He knew, as well as she did, the fantasy was ending.

"Don't you have customers?"

"I've cancelled for the next few days. I'd like to show you Reykjavik. We can go up a day early, tomorrow."

Annie's head ached from holding back her tears so many times. "All right. That would be nice."

That night Kjartan sat paying the bills in his downstairs office. Annie stood in the doorway, wondering if she should do it now or wait until later. There would never be a good time.

She tried to treat it lightly. She handed him her credit card. "Here."

She was unprepared for how much pain she saw on his face. She turned away quickly, leaving the credit card on his desk.

He caught up with her in the hall. Without a word he opened

her hand and pressed the card into it. He pivoted and strode back to his office.

Annie stood there, head throbbing, eyes burning with unreleased tears. She pocketed the card and retreated to her cottage. She had packing to do.

She couldn't bring herself to go back to the house. She wasted as much time as she could folding and refolding her clothes. She took a shower. Read through the tourist information Kjartan had left for cottage guests. Re-read sections of the guidebook. The sun set earlier each night, and by 11:00 the sky was noticeably darker than it had been when she first arrived.

How many months ago was that? she wondered. How could so much happen in such a short space of time?

She waited, knowing he wouldn't come to her. She stood at the door of her cottage several times, almost ready to turn the knob, but then sat back down on the futon and tried to think of other things.

You're wasting a night, she scolded herself. You don't have a night to waste.

She went to bed. She stared at the wall.

100, 99, 98...

Sleep wouldn't come. Not while she slept alone.

She crept into the house, almost certain she would turn and retreat at any moment. Her feet creaked on the stairs. *Shouldn't we turn and run? Isn't this dangerous? What about your heart?* She cracked open the door to his bedroom. Kjartan was asleep.

Annie slipped into the bed beside his and silently covered herself with the blanket. She barely breathed.

Gently Kjartan wrapped his arm around her and pulled her close. Annie couldn't resist. She burrowed against him, grateful for the strength and safety of his arms.

"Don't worry," he whispered, "I won't ask you anything."

"Okay," she said, the hot tears finally spilling down her cheeks. "Good night."

This was Reykjavik as he always thought of it: crowded, loud, everybody and everything so close in, no space to breathe.

But in its way it was beautiful. Brightly-colored houses—reds, yellows, greens—made to cheer the eyes when winter was at its worst. Shops selling furs and tools and computers. Buses ferrying both rich and poor from one end of the city to the other, at regular, predictable intervals. So many restaurants, from the ones serving classic Icelandic dishes to the ones offering Danish and German and Chinese food. There were even a few Mexican restaurants, and that's where she dragged him.

"You don't know how I've been dying for this. Salsa is one of my five food groups."

"There's nobody eating there."

"More for us. Come on."

She was trying to be fun—he could see that. It hurt him all the more. The same gray cast lay over both of them, but neither wanted to call attention to it. They were two lovers on holiday in the capital, nothing on their minds but having a good time.

If she wouldn't look at him that way it would be easier. But he could see her heart was choking.

She ordered for them: lobster fajitas, chips and guacamole, a side of beans, two chicken tacos.

"Not quite right," she whispered so the waitress wouldn't

hear, "but not bad. They think enchilada sauce is salsa, but it's still pretty good." She took another bite. "Do you like it?"

He smiled wanly. "*Já*. It's good."

He wanted to reach for her hand, but didn't want to upset her. When he'd tried it on the street she pulled away and swiped at a tear.

After lunch they wandered back to the street of shops, moving slowly, sometimes brushing arms, talking very little.

"I want to take you to a show tonight," he told her.

"A show? Will I understand it?"

"Yes. It's in English. I think you'll like it."

"All right. That would be nice."

They were so civilized he wanted to shout. He reached for her hand again, and this time held on when she tried to pull away. Her eyes met his. He couldn't let her go on like this.

"Annie..."

"Don't say anything, please." She averted her gaze to the side-walk but held fast to his hand.

He settled for, "Do you want to stop for coffee?"

He found a café where they could sit outside. The weather wasn't cooperating—it was sunny, warm, exquisite. His mood demanded gray skies and rain.

Annie drew in a deep breath. She lifted her chin and looked him in the eye. "I don't want it to be like this."

"I don't, either."

"Let's just pretend—" She stopped herself, shook her head, smiled. "We have a day and a half left. Let's be happy, okay?"

"Okay."

She slipped her fingers under his and stroked her thumb across the top of his hand. "I would love to see a show tonight. What time is it?"

"Seven o'clock."

"Then we have lots of time. Let's check in at the hotel."

She laughed when she saw the sleeping arrangement: two twin beds pushed together. "Even the hotels are like this? No wonder there are only a few hundred thousand people in Iceland. How does anyone make babies here?"

"Let me show you."

. . .

THE SAGAS IN ENGLISH, proclaimed the poster outside the theater.

Annie's smile was the first genuine one she had felt for days. "For me?"

"For you."

It was a one-woman play telling the story of the great saga heroine Gudridur. Annie remembered her well—she was the woman whose obsession with Vinland led to the pre-Columbus discovery of America. She was beautiful, brave, iron-willed. And traveling with her to Vinland was a woman of equal courage:

Gudridur's sister-in-law, Freydis.

The actress portrayed Gudridur as a wide-eyed optimist. She played Freydis as dour and angry. Every time the actress slipped into her Freydis role, Annie leaned forward on her seat. She wanted to hear every word, memorize every gesture. This, finally, was her hero in the flesh.

When Freydis confronted the natives of Vinland and bared her breast, Annie waited for the slap of the sword. Instead, Freydis lifted her bosom and sliced the sword beneath it.

"No!" Annie whispered to Kjartan. "She didn't cut it off, did she?"

"Some people say so."

Freydis collapsed, imaginary blood spilling from her wound. Gudridur rushed to her friend's side, both awe and revulsion written on Gudridur's face. Annie felt the same way. While she admired Freydis' courage, she questioned the need for self-mutilation. In fact, the whole play portrayed Freydis as a woman haunted by self-loathing and destructiveness. Gudridur, on the other hand, maintained an unshakable optimism through every hardship—the death of several of her husbands, shipwrecks, plagues, dangers on the high seas and in the new world.

That was a heroine to be admired, Annie decided. Freydis was just a little too...crazy.

Kjartan seemed pleased to hear it on the way back to the hotel. "Gudridur has always been my favorite."

"How did you know about this play?"

174

"Every summer there are saga shows for the tourists. I never went to one before." He smiled sadly. "I never loved a tourist."

Annie wove her fingers through his. They walked in silence for several blocks. When she was sure she could keep her voice steady, she asked, "What do you think we should do?"

"I have some ideas. What do you want to do?"

Stay here. Love you. Marry you. Make blond children with you.

"I don't know. I'm not sure what's possible. Are you really going to California in October?"

"Yes. I can come see you then."

"I have two weeks off at Christmas. Maybe I could come back here."

"Okay."

"And then I have time at spring break..." The futility of it weighed heavily on her heart. She stopped and leaned against the nearest storefront wall. She dared to look in his eyes. "Is this what you want?"

Kjartan lifted her hand to his lips. He opened her palm and kissed the center of it tenderly. "*Nei*. This is not what I want."

"I WAS KIND OF HOPING you wouldn't be on that plane."

Annie shrugged sadly and accepted her cousin's embrace. "Ugh. What have I done?"

Shannon leaned back and surveyed Annie's troubled face. "Left some heart behind, I'm guessing."

"I was just with him," Annie checked her re-set watch, "two hours ago, Icelandic time. How can I be here already?"

"Did you make a mistake?"

"The whole thing was a mistake." Annie's stomach clenched. "No, that's a lie. It wasn't a mistake. The whole thing was absolutely right."

"Then why are you here?"

Annie hunched under the strap of her bag. She felt tired from sitting cramped for six hours. It was 6:00 PM by her wristwatch, 11:00 PM by her internal clock. She should have been in bed. She should have been nestled in his arms.

Annie sighed. "What can I do? That's not my life."

"Says you."

Dinner was simple—chicken salad, chunks of melon, warmed bread from the bakery.

"Oh, Shan, you don't know how good it feels to crunch something." Annie heaped romaine and melon onto her plate.

"The food was that bad, huh?"

"The fish there is wonderful—as fresh as picking an apple off a tree—but they're not big on fruits and vegetables. They have to grow it in greenhouses, or ship it from Europe. So it's mostly canned stuff."

"No wonder you look so scurvy."

"I do not."

Shannon smiled. "Actually, you don't. You look great. But I don't think it was the food."

Annie stumbled past the implication. "What I really missed was this." She poured more salsa onto her plate and dipped a chunk of bread in it. "I didn't realize how much my body depends on it."

"One of the five food groups," Shannon confirmed. "Six, if you count chocolate."

Annie chuckled. "I made Kjartan go with me to this Mexican restaurant in Reykjavik yesterday—was it yesterday?" she sighed. "Where am I?"

"Icelandic Mexican—that must have been an adventure."

"It wasn't bad, but they don't understand salsa. They need a few million jars of this."

"Maybe you should become an exporter." Shannon stood and cleared the plates. "Ice cream?"

"Mm. Another thing I haven't had in a while."

"I would have thought that's all they served. *Ice*-land."

"Yeah," Annie teased, "they pull it straight from the streams."

She took a few bites of sundae before pushing the bowl away. The length and emotional toil of the day were finally catching up to her. She wanted to stay awake until her normal bedtime, hoping to get back on schedule right away. But then she thought of Sophie and Guy, telling her in their lovely French accents, "If you are tired, you should sleep."

"Okay," Annie said, "I admit it. I'm about to fall face down. I think it's time for bed."

"You haven't told me." Shannon peered at her knowingly. "You've been very good about not telling me all evening."

Annie's voice was soft. "What should I say?"

"That you love him."

"I barely know him."

"But you do—love him."

Annie bit the inside of her cheek. "Last night he asked me to marry him. Can you believe it?"

"Of course I can believe it. And so tell me again why you're here?"

"Because things don't work that way."

"Yes they do," Shannon countered, "all the time."

"Not for me."

She heard herself say it, but imagined another woman, another voice. Freydis, with the down-turned mouth, the cynical sneer, the bitter heart. *Not for me. Nothing good comes to me.*

Annie shook off the image. "If I don't go to bed now you're going to have to carry me."

"Chicken. You just don't want hear what I have to say."

Annie was too spent to rise to the bait. "It was all just a dream anyway. I'm sure we'll both wake up tomorrow wondering how it all happened."

"I know how it happened. It was finally your turn to fall in love."

"Good night, Shan."

"Good night, chicken."

Shannon's guest bed was spacious and empty and cold. Annie settled onto the wide, queen-sized mattress and lay there unwilling—unable—to sleep. If she fell asleep, let go of her hold on the day, it would all be over. She would be firmly, irrevocably, back in her old life.

Finally exhaustion overcame her, and she slept a few fitful hours. She awoke before dawn. She crept down the dark stairs toward the kitchen, and made her first pot of dark, familiar American coffee. Then she padded to the living room and settled into Shannon's reading chair. She propped up her feet, sipped from her mug, and dreamed of another land.

Eventually she heard Shannon come down the stairs, shuffle into the kitchen, and pour herself some coffee.

"How long you been up?" Shannon asked sleepily. She sipped from her mug. "Oo, a long time, I'd say. This is overcooked. How'd you sleep?"

"Not."

Shannon started a new pot of coffee and retreated up the stairs. She returned a few minutes later holding a sheet of paper.

Fresh coffee in hand, she sat on the couch next to Annie's chair and curled her feet under her. Then she handed the paper to Annie.

"What's this?"

"I couldn't sleep last night, either," Shannon explained. "So I spent some time on-line."

Annie's eyes burned with sleeplessness. She tried to focus on the words, but resisted their meaning. She dropped the paper onto her lap. "Shan, I don't understand..."

"Man, how tired are you?"

"Dead."

"Good," Shannon said with a smile. "Then you should be able to sleep on the trip over this time."

Annie's hand shook as she lifted the sheet of paper once more. She stared at the words and numbers until their mystery revealed itself.

It was an itinerary. Minneapolis to Reykjavik, leaving 5:30 PM the following night.

"Sorry," Shannon said, "but things haven't been so good at the firm. I could only afford one way."

Annie shook her head. "Honey, I can't."

Shannon pulled a small bottle from the pocket of her robe. "Here, smell this."

Puzzled, Annie unscrewed the top and lifted the bottle to her nose.

"Cinnamon oil," Shannon said. "They say airplane air is the worst. I don't know—a double dose in such a short time—"

"I'm not going—"

"You should dab a little of that oil under your nostrils every half hour or so—that's what my aromatherapist says. Should keep the heeby-jeebies out of your system."

Annie gazed lovingly at her cousin. "I can't." Tears threatened to lubricate her tired, dry eyes. "That's not my life." She handed the paper back to Shannon. "I hope you can get a refund."

Shannon set her coffee mug on the floor. She leaned toward her cousin and laid her palms on Annie's knees. "No," she said, "not this time. I'm not going to let you do this anymore."

"Shan, I can't."

"You can. You just don't know how to start." Shannon drew a deep breath. "Okay, look, I need to tell you some truth. You're a good girl, Annie, but you're way too good. Don't you think maybe it's time to do something for yourself? Wouldn't that be different." Shannon tempered her sarcasm. "Look, I'm only saying this because I know you won't say it to yourself. When your mom died—"

"Oh, don't—" Annie bent her head and fought off tears she was tired of crying. She knew what Shannon would say—the same thing she had said before: that Annie should have hired a nurse. That she should have called her brothers and told them to come home and do their part. That she should ask them to help her with the medical bills. That Annie had taken on too much, and for what? To prove she loved her mother?

"When she died," Shannon persisted, "I really didn't know what you would do. I thought you might leave Tucson finally— maybe move up here and pal around with me."

Annie thought she knew where this was going, but now she wasn't sure. The slightest hint of a smile escaped. "You know I can't move here. We'd never stop eating."

"True. But I thought it might be good for you—getting out of Dodge. But I didn't say anything—I know how you are. I know you need things to be your idea or you'll never change. You don't like being bossed."

"I get that from you."

"Annie, look at me."

Annie lifted her weary eyes.

"I loved your mom—you know that. But I couldn't help

thinking when she died...don't hate me, okay? But I thought, 'Now's her chance.' All those things I tried to get you to do—come bum around Europe with me, go to college out of state, take a job anyplace but Tucson—you always told me you didn't want to, but I never believed you. I think you stayed because of your mother. That's true, isn't it?"

"I don't know, maybe. But I'm not sorry I did. I like Tucson."

"Yeah, but there are other nice places, too, and you've never bothered to go see them. Now you get this wild hair and go off to Iceland and *ta-da!* what do you find? Someone loves you. You love him. It's not so out of the question. People find each other all the time. That's how this whole thing works."

"But how? I barely know the man."

"So go back and get to know him."

Annie groaned in exasperation. "Everything's so easy for you."

Shannon laughed. "No, it's not. But I don't see the point in doing something stupid just because that's how you've always done it. You're free now, Annie, whether you wanted to be or not. It's time to break out and have a life of your own."

"I do have a life. I have a job. And if I'm not back there in a few weeks—"

"Then what? They'll send a firing squad?"

"The truth is I tried to quit, okay? I took your advice, I sent the letter, but it didn't work."

"What do you mean it didn't work?" Shannon shook her head in amused perplexity. "You say 'I quit' and then you stop showing up. They get the message eventually."

"He wouldn't let me quit. It's too close to the semester."

Shannon threw back her head and growled. "Annie, Annie." She clutched her cousin's knees. "Where did I go wrong with you?"

Annie pulled Shannon's hands away. "Just drop it, all right?"

"Okay, fine. But let me be your lawyer for a minute. Do you remember telling me last year that you had to cover another teacher's classes for the first week of school?"

"Yes."

"And why was that?"

"She got another offer."

"That's right. The day before school started she got an offer from another school. And she took it, right?"

"Right."

"And the world kept spinning, right?"

Annie glowered at her. "Yes."

"You are legally entitled to have a happy life, Annie. You do not have to go back to that school. I looked at the contract. You're a free agent."

Annie stared at her silently for a moment. Shannon stared back. It was a game Annie knew well, and she would not be the one to break.

"I have to go back home."

"Why?"

"I have to take care of the house."

"I'll get someone to forward your bills. The house will keep."

"I have to pack."

"Pack what?"

"My books, my clothes..."

"Annie, you live in Tucson. You wouldn't have the right clothes for Iceland anyway."

Annie broke first. She couldn't help but smile.

"Look," Shannon said, "after what happened with my fabulous whirlwind marriage you'd think I'd be the last person to tell you to jump into this. But you're not like me. You've always had better judgment. I think you need to go with it, Ann. I think your head doesn't lead you astray."

Annie sighed. "But what do I do about the winter? It's dark—do you understand? Dark. What if I go nuts?"

"So you go for a few months, and when you can't stand it any more you make him come back for a few weeks to help you water your plants." Shannon grinned. "Plus, that'll give me a chance to meet him."

"You have it all figured out, don't you?"

"Do you love him?" Shannon asked.

"Yes."

"Can you imagine yourself married to him?"

"Honestly? Yes."

"Okay." Shannon snatched the itinerary from the floor. "Now, didn't you say there was a bus that could take you from the airport?"

ALREADY THE BOOKINGS WERE DWINDLING. A few riders were passing through in the next few weeks, but the frenzy of the tourist season was coming to a close. He would let Petra go soon, and ask her not to come back. From the way she had been acting lately, he suspected she wouldn't object. By September Kjartan would be back to work full time as a horse breeder and trainer. But for now he had at least one more guest.

Someone named S. Wilkinson from the law firm of Duffy, Minder & Brady requested accommodations for two weeks. "I will be traveling with lots of heavy baggage," the e-mail warned. "Please send someone sturdy to pick me up at the bus stop."

Another high-maintenance American.

Nothing at all like the last one.

But when he pulled into the store parking lot, he saw that he was wrong—she was exactly like the last one. Except she had more baggage this time.

She sat where he had found her that first time, dressed in the same red fleece coat and jeans, looking just as weary—but much happier to see him.

She didn't leap to her feet, race into his arms, pledge her endless devotion. She stayed where she was and regarded him sleepily. "Hi."

Kjartan took his cue from her. For whatever reason, she wanted to take this slow. He could do that. His heart pounded against his chest, he wanted nothing more than to scoop her into his arms and taste her lips, but he would wait and give her whatever time she needed.

Kjartan leaned against the van and performed his best imitation of a relaxed man. "Hello. What are you doing?"

"I came back."

"I see that. What's all this baggage?"

Annie patted the box she was sitting on. "A case of salsa. I figure that will hold me for a while." She lifted her foot. "Look, I got slip-on boots. Those other ones were driving me crazy. I brought coffee, too. And Shannon lent me some of her winter gear. I promised her I'd send it back before the first blizzard hits Minnesota."

"Shannon," Kjartan repeated. "Is she S. Wilkinson?"

"Yes."

"Will she be staying for two weeks?"

"No, sorry, that was a lie so you would come to pick me up."

Kjartan's heart thudded. He had to know, but he was afraid to ask.

"How long will you stay?"

Annie made an elaborate show of ciphering—counting on her fingers, muttering calculations. Finally she squinted up at him. "How long do you want me?"

Kjartan pushed away from the van and closed the distance between them. Annie stood and met him half way. Kjartan gathered her into his arms and held her close, breathing in the scent of her hair, of her skin. Their bodies relaxed against each other, pieces of a puzzle finding their right grooves. She kissed him deeply, sweetly, warming him from heart to head.

"I love you," Annie said. "I came back to tell you that."

Kjartan understood how grave the admission was. He cupped her face in his hands and kissed her delicately, protectively. "Annie, I love you, too. Will you really stay?"

She swept a tear from her cheek. "I thought we'd start with at least a winter," she said. "See how things go."

Kjartan held her at arm's length. "That could be a problem."

Annie's face fell. "Why?"

"Our winters last a very long time."

Annie stroked her finger down his cheek. "How long?"

"Sometimes many, many years."

"Okay," she answered. "Good."

ANNIE'S AND SHANNON'S STORIES
CONTINUE...

FIRE AND ICE
(Hearts on Fire, Book 2)

SHANNON IS SMART, competitive, and skilled at her job as a litigator. What she isn't so skilled at is choosing the men in her life.

Annie's new brother-in-law, Thorsten, seems to be everything Shannon wants: charming, athletic, funny and quick-witted. So the smart thing to do is stay as far away from him as she can.

But Thorsten has other plans.

Can two people experienced at the game of seduction surrender to the possibility of love?

~

Available now in ebook and paperback.
https://www.robinbrande.com/books/fire-and-ice/

~

ABOUT THE AUTHOR

~

Robin Brande is an award-winning author, former trial attorney and law instructor, martial artist, yoga instructor, teacher, entrepreneur, and certified wilderness medic.

She writes in multiple genres, including romance, fantasy, young adult, science fiction, and nonfiction.

~

Find out more:
www.robinbrande.com

www.ingramcontent.com/pod-product-compliance
Lightning Source LLC
Chambersburg PA
CBHW050532190726
48284CB00003B/1046